Many Shades of Marriage

Reflecting respect, friendship, and compassion!

By

Prapulla & Dr. Mythri Ramachandra

ISBN 979-8-89498-833-7

Souls did intertwine

In a house adorned with joy and light,
Two families gather, hearts shining bright.
Laughter and blessings fill the air,
As they celebrate a union is rare.
With love and hope, their wishes blend,
For a future where happiness never ends.

In each other, friends they find,
With shared dreams and hearts aligned.
They laugh, they dance, their spirits soar,
Believing this bond will endure evermore.
Through life's adventures, hand in hand,
Together they'll conquer, together they'll stand.

But soon, differences begin to show,
Egos clash, and tempers grow.
Blame replaces the laughter's sound,
In the space where love was once found.
Their friendship fades, replaced by strife,
Each day a battle, cutting like a knife.

Overwhelmed by duties, they feel confined,
Seeking the selves they left behind.
Responsibilities press, identities blur,
They wonder where the love began to stir.
Lost in the chaos, they question their way,
What went wrong, why did the joy stray?

An old wise lady, with eyes so kind,
Whispers truths to ease their mind.
"You're not rivals but compliments," she said,
"Remove the ego, let love be your thread.
See the friend in each other's eyes,
And watch how the love again will rise."

While getting married, you silently carried,
The ego bug, a burden unvaried.
Like a rude rat, it nibbled away,
The strands of friendship day by day.
Send that bug away, let it be gone,
And the friend strand will bond back strong."

With egos dusted, lenses cleaned,
Love and friendship once more gleamed.
They saw the bond they almost lost,
Realizing the cost of the battles they crossed.
In each other, they found their heaven's sign,
Knowing truly, their souls did intertwine.

Contents

Introduction

Manju Goel

Manju Goel is the visionary Founder-Director of Eduvangelists, a Bangalore-based company dedicated to emotional, social, and mental well-being. Her mission is to build a society of mentally strong, emotionally balanced, and socially active citizens.

Manju enhances lives by teaching essential life skills and driving motivation and personal excellence. She fosters holistic growth through programs on personal effectiveness, well-being, social awareness, life skills, personality development, and career skills. She also conducts impactful welfare programs, bringing extensive experience from corporates, government organizations, educational institutions, NGOs, and community programs.

A lifelong learner, Manju holds degrees in Science and Education, a Master's in counselling and Family Therapy, and a PGD in Corporate Counselling. She is certified in NLP, leadership and executive coaching, wellness coaching, sexuality and body empowerment training, Theatre of the Oppressed facilitation, play therapy, psychodrama, story therapy, art therapy, life coaching, and POSH training.

As an empowerment and transformational coach, Manju helps clients become the best version of themselves, build confidence, and reach their full potential, fostering personal and professional growth. As a psychotherapist, she specializes in adolescent, marital, corporate, emotional, psychological, grief, and geriatric counseling, focusing on enhancing psychological, emotional, physical, and social well-being.

Manju's notable achievements include being part of a Guinness World Record for training 1,297 students on "Body Safety and Body Empowerment" with Faith Foundation.

Committed to being a catalyst for change, Manju guides and motivates individuals and key stakeholders through transformative journeys, ensuring they thrive in the ever-evolving landscape of human relationships and well-being.

Foreword

As a seasoned psychotherapist specializing in marital counselling, I have witnessed the myriad dynamics that shape marriages within India's vibrant cultural mosaic. I have guided many individuals and couples through the intricate maze of human relationships. Each day, my journey with clients traverses a kaleidoscope of relationships where Love, trust, hurt, anger, safety, and companionship weave into a rich tapestry of countless shades. This journey has deepened my appreciation for the complexities and nuances of marriage and relationships. When I first encountered, "Many Shades of Marriage," I was captivated by its insightful exploration of this ancient institution within Indian culture.

Dr. Mythri and Prapulla have masterfully captured the essence of marriage in its many forms and revealed it through stories that resonate with the complexities, traditions, and evolving challenges faced by couples today. Drawing on ancient Vedic scriptures, the evolving roles of families, and the realities of modern relationships, the authors navigate the delicate balance between tradition and modernity with profound wisdom and empathy.

Their work resonates deeply with my observations, reflecting the diverse and multifaceted nature of marriage. The book highlights both the challenges and the beauty of this sacred bond, showcasing the resilience and enduring power of love and commitment. Through the journey of a couple deeply rooted in traditional values yet forging a path of their aspirations, this book explores themes of cultural negotiation, personal fulfilment, and the quest for harmony within marital bonds. Each narrative in Many Shades of Marriage portrays the myriad ways in which couples perceive, embrace, and navigate the institution of marriage—from the exhilarating stages of romance to the sobering moments of decision and the inevitable trials that follow.

Amidst diverse perspectives—from seeing marriage as a source of stability to some fearing commitment and seeking the freedom of an open marriage to viewing it as an avenue for personal growth, healing, or societal validation—the underlying thread woven throughout is the spiritual significance of this ancient union. Beyond societal norms and personal desires, Marriage emerges in these pages as a transformative journey where commitment, Understanding, and mutual evolution pave the way for profound personal and collective growth.

This work is a testament to the enduring power of deep commitment and the potential for transformation within marriage. It challenges us to see beyond the surface, and understand the profound spiritual significance of this bond.

Many Shades of Marriage is a must-read for anyone seeking to deepen their understanding of marriage, whether they are newlyweds, seasoned partners, or those contemplating this significant step. This book by Prapulla and Dr. Mythri is a beacon of wisdom, offering guidance and inspiration to all who embark on the journey of marriage. It is with great honor and admiration that I write this foreword, knowing that readers will find in these pages not only stories of love, and struggle but also the keys to unlocking the true potential of their marital unions. I will rest my pen here, leaving the curiosity for readers to explore the book. May this book inspire you, enlighten you, and resonate deeply with your marital journey.

Manju Goel

24 July 2024

Author's note

When we embarked on the journey of writing "Many Shades of Marriage", we aimed to explore the multifaceted institution of marriage through a kaleidoscope of experiences, emotions, and perspectives. Marriage, as a concept, is not a one-size-fits-all experience; it is as diverse and complex as the individuals who enter into it.

In this book, you will encounter a variety of characters whose lives intertwine through the thread of marriage. From the initial stages of infatuation and the blossoming of love to the decision to marry and the inevitable challenges that follow, each story is a reflection of the myriad ways in which marriage is perceived and lived. Some of our characters see marriage as a solution to financial woes, believing it can provide stability and security. Others view it as a convenient escape from personal responsibility, or even as a social trophy, a means to enhance their status and satisfy their desire for public admiration. Some characters fear the commitment and seek the freedom of an open marriage, and those who enter marriage with the purest intentions, only to find themselves at a crossroads of expectation and reality.

Despite these varying perspectives, the underlying essence of Many Shades of Marriage is to reveal the profound spiritual significance of this ancient institution of marriage. Beyond the surface of societal expectations and personal gratification, marriage offers a unique path for soul evolution. It is in the deep commitment and contemplation shared by two individuals where true growth and transformation occur. When couples engage in marriage as friends and partners, they not only evolve individually but also create a nurturing environment for the next generation, stepping into the background gracefully to let the future take its course.

Marriage, as portrayed in this book, is not merely about free will or the pursuit of pleasure based on transient likes and dislikes. It is about the enduring bond of deep commitment, the willingness to work through differences, and the shared journey towards greater spiritual awareness and maturity. Through the stories of these diverse couples, we hope to illuminate the rich tapestry of marriage, highlighting its challenges and triumphs, and ultimately its power to bring about profound personal and collective growth.

Thank you for joining us on this exploration of the "many shades of marriage". May these stories inspire reflection, understanding, and a deeper appreciation for the complexities and beauty of this timeless institution.

Warm regards,

Prapulla and Dr. Mythri

Authors' Acknowledgment

First and foremost, we extend our heartfelt gratitude to all the digital artists whose stunning images have enriched the pages of "Many Shades of Marriage." Your creativity and talent have brought our story to life in ways words alone could not. We also want to thank the digital experts who have ensured that this book is presented in excellent print quality. Your expertise and dedication to perfection are deeply appreciated.

A special thank you goes to the numerous experts and counselors who generously shared their insights and case studies with us. Your contributions have been invaluable in shaping the authenticity and depth of this novel.

To our family and friends, thank you for your unwavering support and encouragement throughout this journey. Your belief in us kept us going even in the toughest times. To our spiritual circle of friends, we are deeply thankful for the invaluable spiritual dimension you added to our concepts through scriptures. Your wisdom and insights have enriched our work profoundly.

Finally, we express our deepest gratitude to our readers. Your enthusiasm and love for our work inspire us every day. Thank you for joining us on this literary journey.

Warm Regards

Prapulla & Dr.Mythri

1. Love's Uncharted Territory

"Let's explore life with the compass of love."

– Unknown

A golden twilight bathed the calm streets of London in a warm glow. In a small apartment tucked away in one of the city's cozy neighborhoods, friends gathered to celebrate two milestones; the love of Shreyas and Pranati and the achievement of Pranati's convocation of a master's degree. The apartment, adorned with twinkling fairy lights and fragrant blooms, emanated an aura of intimacy and joy. Soft music played in the background, mingling with sounds of laughter and chatter as friends, old and new, came together to honor Shreyas and Pranati. The scent of freshly baked treats wafted from the kitchen, teasing the senses and adding to the homely ambiance. Plates filled with tasty delicacies lined the dining table, inviting guests to indulge in a feast fit for the occasion. As the evening unfolded, glasses clinked in toasts to love and success, each sip, a tribute to the journey that brought Shreyas and Pranati to this moment. Amidst the jovial atmosphere, there was an undercurrent of heartfelt sentiment, a recognition of the significance of the evening's dual celebration.

Pranati, radiant in her joy and accomplishment, mingled with guests, her smile illuminating the room as she shared stories of her academic journey and aspirations for the future. Shreyas, by her side, beamed with pride, his eyes reflecting the depth of his love and admiration for his partner. Shreyas, having already completed his master's degree, had spent the past year engrossed in a project at the prestigious National School of London. However, despite the opportunities that lay before him, he had willingly put his plans on hold, eagerly awaiting Pranati to complete her graduation ceremony. For Shreyas, this year wasn't just a pause in his career; it was a testament to his commitment to Pranati, a gesture of unwavering support as she pursued her dreams. And now, as they walked hand in hand through the streets of Europe, he couldn't help but feel a sense of pride in her accomplishments.

Pranati had worked tirelessly to earn her master's degree, balancing her studies with part-time jobs and extracurricular activities. And as she walked alongside Shreyas, she knew that none of it would have been possible without his love and encouragement. Their journey together had been one of sacrifices and compromises, of joy and triumph. As they prepared to board the next chapter of their lives, they knew that whatever challenges lay ahead, they would face them together, bound by the timeless bond of love and devotion. Shreyas and Pranati, a couple deeply in love, found themselves amidst the bittersweet chaos of winding up their home in Europe before their journey to Bangalore, where their new chapter awaited. Their cozy apartment echoed with laughter and chatter as their young, bubbly group of friends helped pack boxes and teased them about their impending marriage.

Shreyas, amidst the warmth of his friends' company, approached Pranati with a beautifully wrapped gift box in his hand. His friends, sensing the significance of the moment, gathered around, their eyes twinkling with anticipation. Pranati's heart, beating with excitement, she eagerly accepted the box, her mind buzzing with thoughts of what delightful surprise lay within. She had half-expected to find a chic piece of Western attire, perhaps a dress or a designer accessory, given the setting of their European standards. With bated breath and fingers trembling with anticipation, Pranati carefully untied the ribbon and lifted the lid of the box. There was a moment of hushed silence as her eyes widened in astonishment at the sight before her. Nestled within the folds of tissue paper lay a resplendent Kanjeevaram saree, its rich turmeric-yellow adorned with an intricate crimson-red border shimmering with golden zari work. Pranati's breath caught in her throat as she marveled at the timeless beauty of the traditional garment, its elegance a stark contrast to her expectations.

Beside the saree lay a pair of antique red-stoned bangles, their traditional South Indian design adding to the allure of the ensemble. Pranati's heart swelled with emotion as she realized the depth of Shreyas's gesture, his reverence for her heritage, and his unwavering love expressed through the thoughtful gift. As the evening wore on, amidst the banter and laughter, she stood before the exquisite traditional gift given with such heartfelt sincerity, Pranati felt a lump in her throat, thinking that their choices and preferences were chalk and cheese! She yearned to embrace Shreyas's traditions wholeheartedly, to weave them seamlessly into the fabric of their shared life. And yet, a part of her hesitated because she feared losing herself and her identity, and autonomy in the name of tradition.

In that moment of hesitation, Pranati wondered if she could find a way to honor their differences while creating a path that resonated with both of them. As she looked into Shreyas's eyes, brimming with love and understanding, she hoped that their love was strong enough to weather any storm, to transcend the boundaries of tradition and modernity, to create a marriage, uniquely theirs.

The teasing of friends increased after she got the gift and Pranati started blushing. Some friends' comments crossed the dignity boundary. Shreyas found himself growing increasingly silent. His friends' Western notions of marriage clashed with his deeply ingrained beliefs in the Vedic system of Indian matrimony. He listened as they joked about marriage being a ball and chain, a restriction on freedom, and a compromise of personal space. Each jest felt like a stab to his soul, a betrayal of his core values. Unable to bear it any longer,

Shreyas excused himself from the group, citing a desire for a quiet walk with Pranati. As they strolled along the dimly lit streets, he finally found the courage to speak his mind. He took Pranati's hand in his and said, "Pranati, I need to tell you something," his voice tinged with uncertainty. Pranati looked at him, concern etched on her face. "What is it, Shreyas? You seem troubled." Taking a deep breath, Shreyas confessed, "I couldn't bear the disrespect they showed towards marriage, towards us. It goes against everything I believe in, everything I was raised to value". Pranati's brow furrowed in confusion. "But Shreyas, you never seemed this affected before. Why does it bother you so much now?" Shreyas hesitated, searching for the right words to explain his inner turmoil. "I guess... I never realized how much it would hurt to hear those words directed at something I hold sacred. Marriage, to me, isn't just a legal contract or a societal construct. It's a spiritual bond, a union of souls guided by the wisdom of our ancient traditions." Pranati listened, her heart heavy with understanding. She had never seen this side of Shreyas before, the side that was deeply rooted in tradition and spirituality. It was as if she was seeing her boyfriend and her fiancé as two different people, each with their own set of beliefs and values. As they continued their walk, Shreyas shared his vision of marriage with Pranati, painting a picture of a life filled with love, respect, and spiritual growth. And in that moment, amidst the gentle breeze and the soft glow of the streetlights, Pranati found herself at a crossroads, her thoughts swirling in a whirlwind of conflicting emotions as she grappled with the delicate balance between tradition and modernity in her relationship with Shreyas. On one hand, she cherished the freedom and autonomy that the Western lifestyle offered. The West views marriage as a partnership based on equality and individual fulfillment. On the other hand, she understood the importance of honoring Shreyas's deeply ingrained cultural traditions and values, including his reverence for the sanctity of marriage as defined by the Vedic system. With love and acceptance, Pranati took a deep breath, the lump in her throat easing as she made peace with Shreyas's thinking. She knew that the journey ahead would be filled with challenges and compromises, and she also knew that as long as they walked hand in hand, their love would light the way through the darkest of nights, illuminating the path to a future built on mutual respect, understanding, and unwavering devotion. Pranati found it hard to sleep that night.

As the early morning sun cast its gentle glow over London Heathrow Airport, Pranati and Shreyas waited to board their flight to Bangalore. While Shreyas was excited at the thought of joining his family for the upcoming wedding celebrations, Pranati couldn't shake the heavy weight of apprehension that settled in her heart. As they queued up to board, surrounded by bustling crowds and hurried travelers, Pranati couldn't help but feel a pang of sadness at the thought of leaving behind her carefree life in London, where she was surrounded by friends who embraced her free-spirited nature. With each step closer to the departure gate, she felt the pull of family obligations growing stronger, weaving a tangled web of expectations and responsibilities around her. At that moment, a fleeting wish crossed her mind – how she longed for it to be just her and Shreyas, their love, untouched by the complexities of family ties and obligations, a sanctuary of peace and joy amidst the chaos of the world.

At Bangalore International Airport, excitement permeated the air as Pranati's parents and cousins eagerly awaited the arrival of the to-be-wed couple. Amidst the throngs of travelers, they stood out, their faces lit up with anticipation and joy, their hearts brimming with love and excitement. Pranati's parents, Sudha and Sudhir, beaming with pride, held bouquets of vibrant flowers, their eyes scanning the crowd for a glimpse of their daughter and soon-to-be son-in-law. Shreyas had informed his parents and had requested them to receive him at home instead of waiting at the airport. He urged them not to inconvenience his grandmothers, Suvarna and Sumathi, by bringing them along. He said that he preferred to take a cab and reach home.

Meanwhile, across the bustling terminal, Pranati's Bangalore friends orchestrated a surprise welcome worthy of the occasion. With laughter and cheers, they carried champagne bottles and bouquets of fragrant blooms, their enthusiasm contagious as they awaited the arrival of their dear friends. As the doors parted and Pranati and Shreyas stepped into the arrival hall, a chorus of cheers erupted, echoing through the airport. Pranati's parents enveloped them in tight embraces, tears of joy glistening in their eyes as they welcomed the couple back home. Amidst the joyful chaos, Pranati's friends presented the couple with champagne and flowers, their faces alight with excitement. With hugs and laughter, they shared the joy of their friends' impending union, their hearts overflowing with love and well wishes for the journey ahead. At that moment, amidst the warmth of their loved ones' embraces and the jubilant cheers of their friends, Pranati was excited while Shreyas felt embarrassed at the sight of his Bangalore friends carrying champagne bottles and bouquets. While he appreciated their gesture, he couldn't shake the feeling of discomfort at the pompous display as he never preferred to show off!

Feeling overwhelmed by the attention and the clash of cultures, Shreyas excused himself from the group, citing a sudden need to check on something urgent. With a polite smile masking his unease, he hurried towards the taxi stand, his cheeks burning with embarrassment. As he boarded the cab, Shreyas took a deep breath, grateful for the solitude, it offered. As the cab weaved through the bustling streets of the Basavanagudi area of Bangalore, Shreyas couldn't help but feel a sense of relief wash over him. In his parents' home, surrounded by their love and understanding, he knew he would find solace amidst the whirlwind of emotions that enveloped him. As the familiar sights of his neighborhood came into view, he felt a sense of calm settle over him, knowing that after the chaos of the airport, there was a haven of peace waiting for him at home.

The cab arrived in front of his beautiful ancestral home, "PRAKRUTI" (meaning nature). Apt to the name, the home was amidst lush green trees and shrubs. The home garden which almost looked like a mini forest, was the neighbour's envy and owner's pride! Quite contrary to the airport welcome, Shreyas was welcomed in a simple traditional way into his home. His parents, sister, and grandmothers were eagerly waiting near the door to receive him with a ghee-lit lamp and kumkum as a symbol of tradition. As Shreyas came near the door, the servants helped him unload his luggage and he bowed to his grandmothers. He hugged his mom and dad; the tight hug melted the anxiety of their wait! He looked into his mom's eyes and she answered the question hidden in his heart. "I know you, my son. You need your silent home and room for some time. So, I have invited all relatives tomorrow to carry on the other customs that will be planned tomorrow. I know too many people will overwhelm you as soon as you arrive". Shreyas felt incredibly happy to have such an understanding mother. He gave her a tight hug again and thanked her. They moved in with contented, happy hearts!

Deepa and Girish, the retired couple from esteemed software professions, exuded a quiet strength as they navigated the rhythms of daily life. Their home was not just a dwelling but a haven of love and care, where Deepa's mother, Suvarna, and Girish's mother, Sumathi, found solace in each other's company. Suvarna occasionally used to visit Deepa's brother's house in Delhi. But she mostly used to stay here a Deepa's house. Sumathi had three children. Eldest daughter was Indrani, Next was son Girish and the youngest daughter was Nalini. The daughters were married and used to reside in the same city and would visit her frequently. Sumathi used to stay with Girish. Both matriarchs, pillars of wisdom and grace, radiated warmth and affection, their presence weaving strong familial bonds that transcended generations. Laya, the bubbly sister of Shreyas was doing her final year internship in the B.Arch program.

Despite their diverse backgrounds and life experiences, the inhabitants of the house shared a common thread – a deep appreciation for art, music, and spirituality. In the evenings, melodious notes of classical music filled the air as family members gathered to revel in the beauty of artistic expression. Discussions on philosophy and spirituality flowed freely, guided by an open-mindedness that welcomed diverse perspectives and beliefs. Amidst the simplicity of their daily routines, each member of the household pursued their passions with fervor and dedication. Whether it was Laya's love for dance, Deepa's love for painting, Girish's mastery of the sitar, or Suvarna and Sumathi's devotion to their spiritual practices, the house resonated with the vibrant energy of creativity and enlightenment. Shreyas's ancestral home housed peace and harmony and it seemed to whisper tales of love, resilience, and the timeless beauty of a life well-lived. Shreyas was wondering, "How will we bridge the differences in preferences and culture between the two homes?"

2. I Expand to WE

> *"As two lives unite in a wedding ceremony, hearts swell with love, eyes glisten with tears, and souls are enveloped in the warmth of shared dreams."*
>
> *– Unknown*

At the to-be-bridegroom Shreyas's house, preparations for the traditional South Indian wedding were infused with a deep sense of reverence for Vedic culture. All first circle relatives arrived abiding by the invite. The family gathered at dawn for a sacred Ganapati Pooja, invoking the blessings from Lord Ganesha to ensure a smooth and auspicious ceremony. The air was filled with the fragrance of fresh jasmine and sandalwood, while the sounds of Vedic chants resonated throughout the home. Elders imparted wisdom and blessings to Shreyas, as he donned his traditional silk dhoti and angavastram (a silk stole), symbolizing purity and sanctity. The house was adorned with vibrant kolams (Geometric designs drawn in front of deities in Indian culture that are considered auspicious) and plantain leaves, creating a divine ambiance reflecting their devotion to age-old customs and spiritual traditions. With hearts full of gratitude and anticipation, Shreyas and his family prepared to leave for the wedding hall, carrying forward the legacy of their rich cultural heritage.

At the to-be-bride Pranati's house, wedding preparations were marked by a lavish and modern approach, blending contemporary elegance with traditional elements. The home buzzed with activity as a team of professional makeup artists, hairstylists, and photographers ensured every detail was picture-perfect. Pranati's designer lehenga, intricately embellished with crystals and gold thread, hung ready for her transformation into a modern-day princess. The scent of exotic flowers mingled with the aromas of gourmet catering, and the decor featured a sophisticated palette of whites and pastels, highlighted by chic floral arrangements and ambient lighting. Friends and family sipped on mocktails and enjoyed the exotic food as they prepared for the day's festivities. Amidst the glamour and excitement, Pranati's family prepared to leave for the wedding hall, ready to celebrate in a style that reflected their opulence and contemporary sensibilities.

Pranati's family settled down at the wedding hall and they were all set to receive the bridegroom's family. They greeted bridegroom Shreyas's traditional team with a contemporary flair. The entrance to the venue was adorned with a stunning fusion of modern floral arches and twinkling fairy lights, setting the stage for a grand welcome. Pranati's friends and family, dressed in elegant attire, lined up to receive the guests with a vibrant mix of traditional aarti (ghee-lit lamps) and modern music. They offered a warm, joyful reception, combining the timeless charm of traditional rituals with the excitement of contemporary celebrations. The atmosphere was electric with the harmonious blend of old and new, symbolizing the union of two families honoring their rich heritage while embracing the present.

Deepa was especially welcomed by Pranati's mother Sudha. Deepa was struggling to contain her joy. It was after all her most loved son's wedding. Months of preparation had made her aging bones creak. The much-awaited day had arrived. The thought of managing multiple relatives, some with a critical eye for everything, some with massive egos, some picky, some doubtful, some too optimistic, essentially humans. Handling unasked-for and well-intended, implausible suggestions had almost driven her crazy. Her husband, Girish, was a stoic philosopher who saw that every moment, even the most joyous was fleeting and was enjoyed as a detached observer. He was awarded the title of the most balanced gentleman ages ago by both sides of the family. He could not be bothered by day-to-day nitty gritty details. He had decided his role for the wedding. Welcome all with a warm smile and send them to the dining hall.

Laya was engrossed in a dream world of pretty clothes, and fun rituals like sangeet. Deepa had her mother, Suvarna, and mother-in-law, Sumathi for support. Both the ladies were staunch believers in duties. They were raised in times when both men and women understood the roles they were taking on as adults and were trained properly to shoulder the responsibilities of a growing family. Over time, they had not left out any opportunity to remind Deepa about training her children to take on additional responsibilities as they grow into adults.

Sudha was a free-willed homemaker who had slogged to come out of the clutches of her rigid mother-in-law and Sudhir was a hard-core chartered account. Pranati was an artist, grew up in many places as her father's job was transferable, studied in a college with heavy Western influence, and was overloaded with information. She was too young to contemplate what she read, validate, and decide for herself. The idea of freedom for all appealed to her, but had no clue what it translated to in real life. She also had friends who believed in questioning everything traditional. None of them had bothered to seek and find answers to their questions sincerely. Questioning was their birthright and they did not hesitate to use the right anywhere.

The wedding hall buzzed with a vibrant and diverse mix of people, each adding to the rich tapestry of the celebration. Elders in traditional silk sarees and dhotis exuded grace and wisdom, their presence a living connection to the past. Young women, adorned in contemporary yet culturally inspired attire, moved gracefully, balancing tradition with modernity. Children darted about in festive outfits, their laughter and energy infusing the air with joy. Friends and extended family members, some dressed in Western attire, mingled freely, their friendship reflecting the inclusive spirit of the event. The ambiance was alive with the sounds of classical Carnatic music, mingling with the hum of conversation and the aromatic scent of jasmine flowers and sandalwood incense, creating a harmonious blend of cultural reverence and joyous celebration.

Sumathi noticed Pranati's lack of enthusiasm for the rituals. When she asked Pranati's mother, Sudha, she learned that modern young women often do not prioritize rituals. This troubled Sumathi, who believed in doing things wholeheartedly. She thought that without conviction, there is no joy, leading to fault-finding and wasting everyone's time, money, and effort. Wisely, Sumathi kept her opinions to herself and trusted in God to guide her family.

The wedding day began with friends constantly questioning the priest about every detail, their attitude coming off as jarring and arrogant. The humble desire to understand and the courage to seek truth seemed absent in these Google-enlightened young people. To them, the Sanskrit mantras were mere jargon, dismissively referred to as cow herders' chants by invaders(British). The elders remained silent, respecting the priest's authority over the rituals.

The priest, a young scholar educated both in scriptures and modern ways, handled the situation with composure. A smile never left the priest's lips. He asked the friends' group to hold their questions as time was running short, and the elders were eager for lunch after the muhurtham (the auspicious timing or moment chosen for the bridegroom officially grasping the bride's hand and tying the knot). With a smirk, the friends began listing their questions. Pranati felt unhappy when her father gave her hand in marriage. A vague question arose in her mind, "Am I a piece of property to be given away in marriage?". Why was she the one wearing a mangalasutra (meaning sacred thread; a sacred necklace that the groom ties around the bride's neck during a Hindu wedding ceremony, symbolizing their marriage and the groom's commitment to the bride) and toe ring? Could she not get married in a crop top? Why the heavy saree? Despite her frustrations, she decided to let go of her choices for a few hours, and that made her parents happy, so she complied.

The young priest focused on his mantras, sincerely ensuring every ritual was followed precisely. He was pleased to see Shreyas's curiosity about the wedding rituals. Shreyas respected the traditions associated with marriage, having seen many happy couples in his family.

As the priest explained each mantra's meaning, Shreyas began to grasp the depth of the marriage institution. He saw his role evolving into that of a family man (*Grihastha*), a provider not only for his family but for society at large. He aspired to truly become a gentleman, embodying fairness, generosity, and the personal sacrifices needed to raise children and help those in need. His heart swelled with gratitude toward the older generation for paving the way. He wondered where he would be if his father had neglected his duties, recalling the many nights his parents cared for him during illness and exams. Pranati, too, got drawn into the conversation. Until the wedding day, she had only thought about her affection for Shreyas and spending her life with him, not the broader institution of marriage. She realized it was not just for her security but the powerful role of nurturer. Doubts arose: Could she handle the role well? Could she stay true to her conscience? Did she have the strength and courage to be fair? Would they remain friends forever? The mantras emphasized friendship in marriage. She decided she needed further discussions with the priest and planned to meet him regularly to understand her role better.

Shreyas was lost in the beauty of the mantras (sacred words, sounds, or phrases repeated in spiritual practices, such as meditation or rituals, believed to have spiritual power and positive effects on the mind and body), while Pranati pondered her new roles. Now it was time to tie the knot. As Shreyas tied the knot, a profound shift occurred in Pranati's mind, blending her free-spirited nature with embracing her new traditional home. In that sacred moment, the depth of the centuries-old rituals resonated deeply, instilling a newfound sense of respect and connection to the customs she now shared with Shreyas. Her heart was swollen with excitement and reverence, appreciating the strength and continuity of the traditions surrounding her. Pranati envisioned weaving her modern values with the rich cultural fabric of her new family, creating a harmonious balance that honored her individuality and the timeless heritage of her new home.

After the wedding ceremony ended, the young crowd, a mix of Western, Indian, and Indo-Western origins, bombarded priest Vinay Shastry with questions that were most rooted in the invaders' interpretation that Indian men had subdued women for centuries and that the West's ideas were now breaking these shackles. They felt a pseudo-pride and superiority from teasing someone they thought was not worldly-wise, not English educated, and a museum piece to have reverence for age-old traditions. Some made fun of his traditional dhoti, and few commented on his long hair. Overall, it was time-pass fun for the Google-enlightened crowd!

As they started heading to the dining hall, Vinay Shastry, took the nearby microphone and announced, "So young friends, please come and assemble here. You had many questions, but I was busy with the rituals. Now, I am all yours. I am fascinated listening to your esteemed opinions about Indian marriage!". He gave a bright smile. His flawless English made a few nervous. The self-proclaimed, know-it-all crowd became alert, and some with conscience regretted their earlier statements. Vinay Shastry made them all sit on chairs and started a brief class on the significance of Vedic marriage. Relatives and friends, who were getting ready to walk towards the dining hall, came back and stood to hear what Vinay Shastry had to say. Curiosity was very much in the air.

Vinay Shastry addressed the crowd and asked, "Let me first understand, what is marriage according to you?" Initially, no one was as eager to answer as they had been to question him. Most were voices reeking of prejudice and lacked any serious contemplation on the subject. Vinay then pointed to each person who had asked a funny question and handed them the microphone to answer. The atmosphere grew serious.

One of Shreyas's friends, Smitha, who was born in India but raised in the West, answered, "I am scared of the concept of marriage in India. I've seen how women are exploited and dominated, losing their individuality. Married women in India can never make their own decisions. They have to stay with in-laws, and even if their compatibility with their spouse isn't great, they are forced to fit in. The whole system is flawed!" Another boy stood up and said, "They spend a hell lot of money on marriages, only to regret it later.!" Another girl added, "Marriage is a complicated institution where you invite complexities into your life."

A daring girl stood up, and said, "In India, marriage is a deadly commitment. According to me, you must be free to get in and get out of marriage, as you wish. But I've seen that in India, it's not possible." A middle-aged lady, dressed very gorgeously, stood up and declared, "It is a huge responsibility that will make you age faster." Some of the hardcore Indian crowd shared their opinions as well. They said, "Marriages are made in heaven," "An institution to raise ethical next generation in warm home", "It is the union of two souls," "It is a friendship for a lifetime," and offered many other positive comments as well.

Vinay Shastry asked, "So, most of you share a very negative image of marriage, but I am curious to know why you have come here dressed up so nicely when you don't have a good opinion about marriages, especially Vedic marriage! Your actions don't align with the ideas you have shared." Vinay Shastry continued, "It is so disheartening to see the half-baked knowledge of the youth, who are supposed to be the torchbearers of our culture for future generations! My dear "young know-it-all scholars"! Unfortunately, modern youngsters often prioritize convenience over conviction, leading to the institution of marriage deteriorating. Many enter marriage without understanding the institution and its goals. The contemporary emphasis on individualism, instant gratification, and materialism undermines the profound and enduring values that marriage traditionally embodies. A shift, that has resulted in relationships lacking depth and commitment, focused on only personal comfort rather than mutual sacrifice and growth. As a result, the sacredness and substance of marriage are compromised, leading to increased instability and diminished respect for this vital social institution. It is so sad to see that this trend has metaphorically "painted marriage black," obscuring its true significance and value.

It is high time that you people who are tomorrow's hope, get the concepts right. The Vedic system of marriage, as outlined in ancient scriptures, emphasizes a balanced partnership based on dharma (duty), friendship, mutual respect, and spiritual growth. These texts act as a manual for right living, guiding individuals and society towards harmony and stability. However, over time, individual beliefs and personality limitations are attributed to marriage. Anyone who does not understand the goal and one's role, and associated responsibilities in a marriage, gets into troubled waters. They do not possess the skills or heart to nurture a home with love for the next generation. Prioritizing materialism, social status, or personal gratification over the spiritual and ethical aspects has only caused dissatisfaction on a massive scale. Once the sanctity and purpose of marriage are undermined, conflicts, broken families, and a weakening of the societal fabric are a natural consequence. Instead of owning up to the fact that the roles and responsibilities are not understood and checking one's preparedness to take up the role, marriage is blamed for all individual flaws. The emphasis on dowry, the commodification of relationships, and the erosion of gender roles have further compounded these issues.

Vedic marriage is an institution celebrating the union of two divine souls, willing to share and grow together on their spiritual quest, happy to shoulder the responsibilities of raising the next generation and providing the framework to raise tender children in a safe, secure, warm home. I need not elaborate on the consequences of an insensitive approach to raising children. You are all well-traveled and well-read. I shudder to think of generations raised by insecure, selfish, individuals married only for their convenience. What are we passing on as legacy values to the next generation from our family? Mistrust, insecurity, fear, hatred. By moving away from the original scriptural teachings, the core values that sustain healthy marriages and, by extension, a stable society, are being lost. This trend highlights the need to revisit and realign with the scriptural principles that promote holistic and enduring relationships, thereby reinforcing the societal structure.

Just as an expensive gadget functions optimally when used according to its user manual, human life, which is even more precious, should be guided by the wisdom of far wiser ancestors, captured for posterity in our scriptures. These scriptures, like the Vedas, provide comprehensive guidance on how to lead a fulfilling and righteous life. They offer insights into moral conduct, duties, and responsibilities with every role we play, individual accountability to excel in every role, and the deeper purpose of existence, much like a manual that ensures a gadget's longevity and performance. By adhering to these scriptural teachings, individuals can navigate life's complexities, achieve personal growth, and contribute positively to society. Deviating from these guidelines leads to confusion and misinterpretation, much like mishandling a gadget without following its manual. This deviation can result in a life filled with strife, imbalance, and a loss of direction, affecting both personal well-being and societal harmony. Please read these "user manuals", and clear any doubts so there are no accidents."

He remembered the girl Smitha's comment. He turned towards her and mentioned specifically. "By the way, young lady, I beg to differ from your view that married women are all exploited in India. You have got it wrong! You cannot paint marriage black because of individual ignorance about marital goals. The cultural roots play a big role in fulfilling marital roles. Vedic marriage reveres women as crucial partners in upholding dharma and spiritual growth. They are regarded as embodiments of Shakti, the divine feminine energy, playing a crucial role in maintaining the balance and prosperity of the household. Women are honored as the nurturers and educators of future generations. They are entrusted with the biggest responsibility: laying the foundation for the moral, and spiritual upbringing of children. Mantras highlight the friendship aspect between husband and wife. How can a couple hating each other raise stalwarts of the next generation?" The girl bent her head down and was left with no words to debate back to defend her wrong opinions.

He didn't spare that middle-aged lady who had commented that marriage should be a free-willed and open institution as it is very difficult to take responsibility. He turned towards her and said, "Madam, for your statement I would like to stress the point that Vedic marriage emphasizes friendship as the foundation of the marital relationship, recognizing it as the key to a harmonious and enduring union. Marriage is not merely a social or contractual obligation, it is a partnership rooted in mutual respect, understanding, and companionship. The concept of friendship (mythri) is integral to this bond, where both partners support and uplift each other through life's journey. This friendship fosters open communication, trust, and a deep emotional connection, allowing the couple to navigate challenges and evolve together spiritually. By prioritizing friendship, Vedic marriage ensures that the relationship is built on a solid and nurturing foundation, enhancing the overall well-being and stability of the family unit. It is not a child's play so people can walk in and walk out based on flimsy likes and dislikes! Please understand what you are getting into before getting married. Why jump blindly and blame the well later?"

This deep defending speech full of concern to address wrong ideas about marriage from Vinay Shastry left the crowd speechless! One young English girl in the crowd dressed up in Indian attire to keep up the style of the event, was impressed by his speech and asked, "Mr. Shastry, what is your educational background?". He calmly replied, "I am Dr. Vinay Shastry. I have completed my PhD from Banaras Hindu University, located in Varanasi. It has been the cradle for spiritual studies since time immemorial. I am proud to say that I studied Indian philosophy and Vedanta at BHU.

I travel across the globe today to places like the University of Oxford, and Harvard University, United States where I conduct Indian philosophy and Vedanta classes. Thanks to my Alma Mater." The young entitled crowd who had underrated Dr. Vinay Shastry were dumb stuck! They felt Dr.Vinay Shastry was truly an example to prove that stuff always beats style! Dr. Shastry had successfully enlightened the misguided crowd on the real significance of marriage in one's life. His profound thoughts lingered in everyone's ears in the marriage hall and they felt the goosebumps as they listened to such a knowledgeable man!

They were unable to continue the conversation. Their friends had ordered a huge multi-tier cake for the wedding, attracting a crowd of kids. Shreyas asked, "Do you understand why the cake is cut on wedding day in the West? Till we find the answer, let us have the kids enjoy the cake. We will cut when we know the why". Sumathi and Deepa exchanged smiles. They knew, in their hearts that their home had the right culture and the next generations would be raised with the right values. Shreyas looked into Pranati's eyes and said, "Pranati, welcome to my life as my soulmate.". Pranati was mesmerized. Pranati walked with her husband to see Dr. Shastry off. As they exchanged knowing smiles, Vinay Shastry knew he had Pranati as a new student and many more sincere seekers would follow. On his journey back home, Shastry was preparing a list of books to refer to and the scholars to meet so no question goes unanswered.

3. Nip it in the Bud

"In relationships, you get what you tolerate."

– Unknown

A week-long wedding celebration had left Pranati craving for quiet time alone. She opened her eyes to the early rays of sun streaming through the ornate window next to her bed. The soft humming of a devotional song from Suvarna offering prayers to holy basil plant (Tulasi pooja), the reciting of shlokas as Deepa cooked in the kitchen, and the soft sound of Girish watering the plants took her to an ethereal place. She smiled and got up to be a part of the serene surroundings of her new home. The phone rang and she groaned, "Ah, perfect time for the phone to ring and spoil the solitude!".

Pranati picked up the phone and saw it was her long-lost school friend, Priya, who had missed the wedding and wanted to meet for a leisurely chat. Excited, Pranati agreed and hopped out of bed to get ready. As she sang her way to the kitchen, Deepa informed her that the family planned to visit their native village to seek blessings for the newlywed couple.

Pranati found herself in a dilemma, torn between her promise to Priya and her family's plans. While not an atheist, she had been looking forward to catching up with her old friend. Ultimately, she decided to be a dutiful daughter-in-law and called Priya to cancel. Deepa noticed Pranati's reluctance and asked, "Pranati, is there any problem? Are you okay with the travel plan?" Pranati reassured her "It is all fine, Amma".

Priya couldn't accept that Pranati was changing her plans. She started with logic, "For how long will you keep prioritizing your family's needs? Yes, it's natural to bend a bit when you're new in the family, but will this become the new you? Will you forget your true nature trying to fit in? What happens to your own beliefs? Isn't this subtle slavery? You're no longer the master of your will. It starts with small requests, and soon your needs will be ignored. You'll be as good as the sofa in the house." A visibly confused Pranati couldn't understand why Priya was being so harsh. Pranati was happy about going to the temple and looking forward to a nice drive with everyone. She told Priya she had to rush and get ready.

For the first time, Pranati donned an elegant silk saree, its rich hues complementing the traditional jewelry that adorned her. As she gracefully descended the stairs, her poise and beauty radiated through the fabric's shimmer. Shreyas, who was loading their bags for the trip into the car, suddenly found himself captivated by the sight of Pranati. He paused, mesmerized by her transformation. The elegance of the saree and the timeless beauty of the traditional jewelry made her look like a vision from his dreams. For a moment, his heart skipped a beat, completely entranced by her allure, and all the hustle and bustle faded into the background.

Girish and Deepa noticed Shreyas admiring Pranati; they silently exchanged knowing smiles. Their hearts became full with happiness, witnessing their son's new phase of life filled with love and admiration. Deepa, her eyes moist with tears of joy, silently prayed that this bond between Shreyas and Pranati would remain strong and enduring forever. She wished for their love to grow deeper with each passing day, nurturing a lifetime of happiness and togetherness. This moment of pure connection between the newlyweds was a cherished blessing for both Girish and Deepa, filling them with immense contentment.

The ride to their native place took a couple of hours. The beautiful idol of the Lord made Pranati forget the conversation she had with Priya. Nobody was forcing her for anything. She had felt like wearing a simple saree as it was appropriate when visiting a temple. Deepa had said, "Pranati, are you sure you will be comfortable in this silk saree throughout the trip? I suggest you get an extra pair of comfortable clothes to change into after the temple visit. We have to trek to another temple uphill". For Pranati, the thoughts of asserting her will and cozy soft care from Deepa clashed again and again in her mind. Pranati got exhausted with her mind and decided to distract herself with the activities at hand.

A nice trek uphill, green rolling hills, a cool breeze, walk with Shreyas made her forget her mind for a while. As they started climbing down, she told Shreyas, "Shreyas, my friend Priya had called. She wanted me to meet her today. But I came to know about this trip later. So I changed the plan". He said, "You made the right decision by prioritizing family needs first, Pranati. I have seen my parents and grandparents shift their preferences to accommodate our needs. I'm sure you have noticed the same in your side of the family. I want to follow the same priority.". Pranati was happy that he valued family.

Pranati, who had earlier never spoken about her family in depth with Shreyas, opened up for the first time. "Shreyas, the scenario in my home is very different. Though my mother is a homemaker, she is not completely home-oriented. We were not staying with our grandparents. At least since the time I grew up, I hardly have any memories of them. Amma says we were together when Pranav and I were kids. Even now, my mother has the final say in pretty much any decision, small or big, in my family. My father has been a busy career-oriented workaholic who would travel extensively. He had no time to spend leisurely with his family. My mother has her circle of family and friends. They go out on trips and have lunches outside and none of them are very traditional. Shreyas, I do not have many memories of huge festival celebrations. My mother has raised me to be independent, do my chores diligently, and decide for myself. She is not clingy or needy. She has her world and is happy. She thinks I now have my own home, confident that I can manage my challenges on my own.". Shreyas said, "Hmm. Guess each family is different." Pranati thought to herself, "I am scared, our families are not even a combination. They are contrasts!"

As they got back home, Deepa started running around to prepare dinner. Pranati suggested, "Amma, all of us are tired. Let us order some food from outside and maybe cook something simple for the elders". Deepa was not for ordering and said, "No, Pranati, I will prepare something simple for all. After travel, let us not eat outside food". Pranati was more than tired and wanted to rest. She saw a clash ensuing inside her. She could not simply walk off to her room, leaving an equally tired Deepa to handle everything. Though her mind rebelled, she decided to help in the kitchen. She was getting more and more tired as tasks piled up. She was scolding herself for not resting. Shreyas was not aware of her state and started, "I do not understand how people can frequently eat outside food. Nothing as soothing as home food, especially post-travel". Pranati was irritated and snapped, "Yes Mr. Choosy, if you find home food so soothing, why don't you come and help in the kitchen?" Shreyas was taken aback. He had not seen this side of Pranati. She was by nature soft-spoken. Shreyas was not someone who expressed his displeasure. He would sulk for days sometimes and get his way. He turned away from her and got into his shell.

As the sun started streaming through the windows, Pranati woke up refreshed and was rearing to go. She suddenly remembered she was rude and curt to Shreyas and wanted to apologize to him. She came down to the kitchen searching for Shreyas. Deepa said, "Good morning, Pranati". Pranati asked, "Amma, where is Shreyas?". Deepa gave a surprised look, "Shreyas left early for the office. He said he had some work. Didn't he tell you while leaving?" Pranati was in a fix. She lied to Deepa, "Maybe I was sleeping, and he didn't tell me." But Deepa's mature eyes caught Pranati's lie. But she kept quiet for the moment. Pranati messaged him that she was sorry for what she said. She explained that she was irritated and tired when he spoke. She was thinking of making it up to him with a nice dish. She got a bit worried as there was no response from him till lunchtime. Pranati was walking like a restless cat in the corridor. She heard the honk of Shreyas' car. She ran down to receive him. Shreyas entered the house, dropped the keys, removed his footwear, and went directly to Deepa, who was arranging her crockery in the dining hall, and pretended he had not even noticed Pranati! He asked Deepa, "Amma, I need a cup of strong coffee". Deepa quipped, "A married son should ask his wife, and not his mother for coffee. He can also make coffee for himself and others too." Shreyas got annoyed, "Will I be getting coffee or shall I go the corner café?" Deepa gave a stern look, "Shreyas, Pranati, if you both have problems, you sort it out between yourselves. Don't pull me in between". Shreyas left for his room upstairs. Pranati ran into the room behind him and repeatedly said, "Sorry, Shreyas. I will ensure that this will not happen again". Shreyas said, "Pranati, I am busy, and do not bother me." Pranati was hurt. She felt like crying out loud; she had not committed a grave sin, like murder.

Shreyas was fuming inside when Pranati expressed something he didn't like. Unused to openly acknowledging his emotions and accustomed to having his way as a pampered child, he had cultivated an image of himself as flawless and infallible, bolstered by his academic achievements and family's deference. Despite genuinely liking Pranati, his ego would not relent easily. Unable to easily surrender to hurt feelings, he decided to teach Pranati a lesson, wanting her to beg for forgiveness before he would consider making peace. In his frustration, he believed she needed to learn not to challenge him, deepening his sulk as he wrestled with his wounded pride and the complexities of adjusting to married life.

Days went by and Pranati was trying hard not to let this small thing become big between them. Isn't marriage about letting go and moving on? If such a small thing could cause so much of a rift, she shuddered to think about years together. She was feeling suffocated. She was clueless about who expected what from her making her shaky within.

Deepa had noticed the rift among the young couple. They no longer laughed together, and avoided having food together; Pranati's long face was hard to miss. Pranati recalled a different Shreyas from their time in London, a memory that brought a warm smile to her face. She vividly remembered an evening when she was upset over a trivial matter, and her frustration had boiled over. Shreyas, with patience, had sat beside her, listening intently without interruption. He had spoken softly; his calm demeanor had soothed her anger. His understanding and empathetic listening had gradually melted her irritation and replaced it with a sense of comfort and security. At that moment, his unwavering support and gentle reassurance had won her confidence and deepened her trust in him. But his extended period of cold reaction now left her clueless.

Sumathi, being the most empathetic and wise, decided to comfort Pranati. She called Pranati to her room. She placed her hand on Pranati's shoulder and asked her, "Dear, what is bothering you? Her soft, kind words brought on dammed tears, and she narrated what had happened. Sumathi sighed heavily. She knew what the poor girl was going through. "Pranati, I understand your state. I know that your loyalty to your husband has stopped you from discussing how you felt after this episode even to your mother". Pranati sobbed and said, "Ajji", and all the other words got choked in her throat. Sumati said, "Pranati when I was like you and I used to feel low in my new home, I did not have anyone to confide in. All the ladies were older and I could not share day-to-day grouses". Sumathi told her gently, "I understand how you feel. I had told Girish and Deepa that Shreyas' attitude would be his biggest obstacle in his life. Sulking does not solve problems. The ego has no place in any family that wants to thrive. It is time for us to take action." Pranati was surprised that Sumathi knew this problem and was relieved she had support.

While Sumathi was consoling Pranati, Girish and Deepa pitched in. Girish said, "Don't worry Pranati, if Shreyas is tough, I am his dad. I will teach you to be tougher!" Deepa added, "My dear new daughter-in-law, please don't be morose. It feels like a grey cloud at home. Just do what I say. Be normal around Shreyas. Do not give his behavior too much importance. Go about your day as if nothing happened. And yes, no need to pacify him. We can see the problem we have created. We will only set it right. As soon as Shreyas sulked, one of us would cave in and take his side. He has not fought his battles with grit, fairness, and by keeping his massive ego aside. His skills have kept him in good standing in his job. Attitude is becoming arrogant and we are scared that he has to pay a huge price if his attitude is not addressed now".

Pranati felt a deep sense of gratitude witnessing how the elders in Shreyas' family approached even minor issues by delving into their roots rather than brushing them aside. This thoughtful approach not only resolved conflicts but also strengthened the bonds between family members. Pranati appreciated how this method fostered understanding and mutual respect, allowing everyone to feel heard and valued. It showed her the importance of patience and thorough communication in nurturing lasting relationships, encouraging her to embrace these values in her interactions within the family. Witnessing the elders' dedication to maintaining harmony through understanding left a lasting impression on Pranati, reinforcing her belief in the power of genuine dialogue and consideration in building strong familial ties.

It was a Friday evening and Shreyas came back from the office. Shreyas was shocked to see Pranati enjoying evening coffee with his family. She pretended as if she did not even notice him! He thought, "How come she is not flustered?" As he entered, people ignored him. That came as a bigger shock. Not even his grandmother asked him what he wanted. He walked towards them and took his coffee. No smile from his always-smiling mother or a joke from his witty father. Pranati did not even notice his presence. He wanted to ask what had happened. Ego rose and he walked to his room in a huff. He thought, "If they ignore me, I can sulk for months. I'm the expert in sulking. One of them will come running after me".

For a week, the same situation continued. Pranati made no effort to pacify him. The only conversation at the dining table was about food. Shreyas was visibly getting upset. He had one close friend, Mukund, who understood him. And had put up with his tantrums since childhood. He called Mukund and related what was happening at home. Mukund was puzzled. His friend was a know-it-all and was averse to taking any sensible advice. Mukund was a calmer person who respected people for who they were and valued their presence in his life. He was grateful for his family and loved to spend time with them. Mukund told Shreyas, "For God's sake, talk to Pranati, Shreyas. She is your wife. Did she not say sorry multiple times? And yes, mean it from her heart? Maybe she is hurt by your behavior and haughtiness. With marriage, the couple's identity is forged, and it is natural to let go. One person cannot have their say in everything at all times. There are decisions to be made daily. One person cannot know everything. Communication is key to understanding the other's standpoint. Both of you want an end to the conflict. Why not think from the other side for a change?". Shreyas had had enough of seeing long faces at home. His was the longest. He wanted his smiling, calm wife back.

For the first time in his life, Shreyas saw he had more to lose by sulking and going with his version of the story. He saw that there were countless times when his mother was tired and still made what he wanted as she wanted him to eat and then go to bed. If only he had adjusted and given her rest? Ego raised another question. How will he manage the fact that he got back to Pranati? Will she not take him for granted henceforth? With all the doubts, he decided to break his nasty habit of sulking. He came home whistling.

He called out to Pranati. "Pranati, I'm sorry I sulked for so long. Yes, it must have hurt you badly. For the first time, I'm saying sorry voluntarily. Since childhood, I have said sorry only when forced by my elders. Never knew it is so easy and feels so light.". He was grinning when he finished. Sumathi quipped, "I was not expecting you to say sorry for at least a month, that too after your father intervenes. I am happy it is only a week." His father added, "My slow coach son is speeding up.". Deepa was relieved that his attitude was changing. Pranati was genuinely thankful to the elders in her family. She decided to discuss serious matters with them and not imagine anything nasty. Without their guidance, she had imagined all sorts of scenarios, including the divorce court. She knew that her marriage would be just fine with their blessings and support. Shreyas decided to genuinely practice apologizing when in the wrong.

Shreyas and Pranati left for a walk in the nice breeze confident about sorting their issues, big and small through goodwill and graceful communication, with respect. Sumathi started reminiscing about her challenges as a young bride and how her father-in-law became her wise counsel. She was happy she continued his legacy of guiding with understanding and stabilizing the foundation for the next generation. Girish and Deepa had learned that their role had changed forever and they had to be fair to all the members of their family, related by blood or not.

4. One Size Fits All?

"One size fits all is not a solution. It is a problem."
– Daniel Quinn.

Sudha and Sudhir were very satisfied and happy that the wedding of their daughter went well. The next morning, Sudha was tired and was relaxing in her garden with a cup of coffee. She had asked Sudhir to get some breakfast from the hotel as she was in no mood to cook. Sudhir said "Madam is looking worried. What happened?" Sudha just nodded and said, "No I am tired that's all." Sudhir left to get breakfast from a nearby restaurant. Sudha was worried about Pranati. Though she had seen that Pranati was married to the boy whom she loved, the fact that they were traditional and culturally rich was triggering a remote fear in her mind which she could not explain to anyone.

Sudha's mind was plagued with a deep-seated fear as she contemplated her daughter Pranati's decision to live in a joint family. Memories of her own experiences resurfaced, where she struggled to find her place amidst the constant scrutiny of in-laws, the demands of a critical sister-in-law, and an overwhelming burden of household chores. The relentless expectations left her feeling suffocated and undervalued, and she dreads the thought of Pranati enduring the same hardships. Sudha's concern for her daughter's well-being fueled a stressful mindset, as she worried that history may repeat itself, leaving Pranati trapped in a cycle of sacrifice and subservience, unable to pursue her dreams and aspirations.

Sudha, getting too scared of her thoughts, called Pranati immediately and enquired, "Pranati are you okay? Is everything in your new home fine?" Pranati said, "All are fine amma. New home, nice people. Ajji is out of the world. Appa and Amma are very warm. Still, I need time to get adjusted." The mother instinct in Sudha started questioning and decided not to budge till she was satisfied with the answers. Sudha continued, "Then tell me how is your mother-in-law with you when you are in her kitchen?" Pranati said, "Amma just chill. I knew Shreyas. Not his family. Even I am new here and you want me to describe people? How is it possible? Please be a little patient." Sudha, in her worry, was not ready to listen to Pranati and cautioned her to watch out for red flags. Sudha said, "The expectation you set as soon as you enter your husband's house, becomes your signature and stays throughout. Don't trust people easily and blindly." A skeptical Sudha told her, "Wait and watch, don't be naïve, and trust everyone with just a few interactions. By nature, I know you are blindly trusting. I have spent years telling you to be cautious. I have seen many wolves in sheep's clothing at close quarters in our family. Because of my past experiences, I felt like telling you Pranati.". Pranati said," Amma, I will call you later. I have to go with Ajji to the terrace garden to pluck flowers for her pooja." Sudha had brought up her children in a fight or flight mode but not in a secure and safe mode! So naturally she was scared.

Sudha got more worried after Pranati hung up the phone. As Sudha was sitting with her thoughts in the garden, Sudhir came in holding breakfast packets and a few vegetables. He noticed Sudha was lost in her thoughts.

Sudhir had become increasingly quiet over the years, withdrawn within his work outside the home, leaving Sudha feeling a tug at her heart for the warm, caring person he was. Sudha's parents initially saw him as a devoted son, earning him the nickname "Shravana Kumara," confident that his caring nature would extend to being a responsible husband. Despite concerns about his mother Rukmini's dominating personality, they trusted Sudhir's good character and his father Srinivasan's influence. Over time, Sudha adjusted to her new joint family, eager to care for everyone. However, Rukmini's demanding ways soon strained Sudha, who married young without fully understanding the dynamics. She found herself fulfilling household tasks as directed by her mother-in-law Rukmini. In contrast, her father-in-law, Srinivasan was affectionate towards her. Sudhir, who was supportive, gradually became focused on his career, leaving Sudha to bear much of the domestic burden alongside raising her children and sometimes even her sister-in-law's child. As tensions mounted and Sudha felt increasingly marginalized, she attempted to confront Rukmini's unfairness, only to be silenced by Sudhir's pleas for compromise. After nearly two decades of silent suffering, Sudha finally stood up against Rukmini's toxicity, prompting a reluctant Sudhir to move them to a separate home. Despite the strained relationship between Sudha and Sudhir, their children remained unaware of the underlying turmoil. Pranati, sheltered from the details of her parents' struggles, grew cautious but found solace and warmth in her relationship with Shreyas. Pranati decided to watch for actions based on her mother's cautionary advice.

One day, Pranati started to her mother's place on a scooter. Deepa saw Pranati taking the scooter through her reading room's window. She left her book and took a helmet from the verandah to Pranati and told: "Drive safely". Pranati was never used to this type of care. She smiled and said, "I am planning to go to Amma's place." Deepa smiled like a friend and that smile conveyed to Pranati that she never wanted an explanation as to where Pranati was going. Deepa said,

"It must be so difficult for Sudha and Sudhir to send you off. I can understand. There is no hurry. Spend your time to your heart's content there. Oh! ok, my online Sanskrit classes are starting and I need to rush inside. Bye Pranati, drive safely. Please ping me once you reach." Pranati's heart was melting but her mind was full of Sudha's advice. There was a clear conflict! While she was riding her scooter, the head and heart conflict blinded her focus on the road and she was lost. She hit a car and fell from the scooter two roads away from the house and had a deep cut on her leg. A few students who were on their bikes stopped and helped her to move to the side of the road. They made her sit on a chair in front of a petty shop and parked her vehicle to the side. An auto guy murmured," These girls are in their dream world and they come to roads by putting their lives and others' lives also at risk. I don't know who gave her license." Pranati felt too ashamed for her negligence on the road.

As Pranati fell off her scooter, she felt a sharp pain in her leg, followed by a hot flush of embarrassment as a small crowd gathered around her. Struggling to hold back tears, she tried to stand but the pain was too much. Distressed, she called Shreyas at his office, and as soon as he answered, she broke down, crying like a small child. Shreyas, hearing her sobs, was filled with concern. Without a second thought, he called Girish and Deepa, confident they would take care of Pranati.

Girish and Deepa, genuinely concerned for Pranati, rushed to the scene. Girish remained calm and composed, his steady presence providing much-needed reassurance. He examined Pranati's leg and assured her it was just a minor injury that could be managed with some first aid. Meanwhile, Deepa, emotional and tender, felt a pang seeing Pranati's wound. Her heart swelled with maternal concern as she helped Girish gently clean and bandage the injury. Pranati saw that they were concerned. Deepa was almost in tears seeing the cut. The whole ride to the doctor's place, Girish was giving instructions on stemming the blood flow. Deepa had got a first aid kit from home. Finally, they reached the clinic nearby and got Pranati treated. The doctor cleaned and dressed up her wound and prescribed anti-inflammatory drugs and painkillers for three days. He advised rest for a week. Girish and Pranati took care of Pranati with the kind of attentiveness reserved for a child, ensuring she felt safe and comforted before bringing her back home.

By the time they reached home, Deepa had already informed Sudha about the incident. Sudha, anxiously waiting, rushed to her daughter's side as soon as they arrived. Pranati, surprised to see her mother, felt a wave of relief wash over her. Deepa, noticing Sudha's worry, expressed her understanding: "I can understand being so anxious myself. Imagine the anxiety of a mother." Sudha, her eyes filled with concern and love, held Pranati close, grateful for the support and care provided by Deepa and Girish. The family united in their concern and love for Pranati, helped her settle in, ensuring she felt surrounded by warmth and reassurance. Sudha was thankful her daughter was taken care of, but the skeptic would not die soon.

Laya said, "Pranati, please rest. I will help Amma with chores and yes, Shreyas had called. He has taken two days off." Seeing the family's connection and concern, the doubt cloud in Sudha's mind slowly started clearing. In a week, Pranati's wound healed.

Deepa and Laya wanted Pranati to accompany them for shopping to select a saree for Laya's final year send-off at college. While Deepa and Laya came down after getting ready, they saw Pranati still in her track pants and tees on a rocking chair reading a book. Laya exclaimed, "Pranati, you are not ready yet? We need to go to buy a saree." Pranati said, "Hey Laya, you and Amma are ready. Please go ahead. I'll not be of much help." Deepa said, "How can we go without you? I can't choose for Laya. You can do justice to shopping. We will wait for you. Get ready and come." Pranati felt that she was important to them. It was a proud feeling. She quickly got ready and came. "How are we going?", asked Pranati. Deepa said, "Our driver is waiting," giving a smile at Girish. Girish got up and said, "It is my pleasure to drive the princesses and the queen in a royal chariot to buy their classic six yards!" Pranati thought Girish had so much time and heart for his family!

As Pranati engaged in the shopping trip with Deepa and Laya, a poignant comparison struck her mind between Sudha and Deepa. Memories of past shopping trips with Sudha flooded back, where Sudha's dominating presence left little room for Pranati to express her preferences. Sudha had always taken charge, never allowing Pranati the freedom to make choices or voice her opinions, making the experience more about following her mother's directives than enjoying the process.

Deepa's approach was refreshingly different. Not only did Deepa involve Pranati in every decision, but she even allowed Pranati to choose the shop they would visit. In the bustling shopping street known as Bridal Street, there was a store called *Queen's Choice*, famous for its exclusive designer collection of grand sarees. Pranati had always wanted to explore this shop, but Sudha had dismissed it, deeming the goods overpriced and not worth the expense.

When Pranati tentatively suggested Queen's Choice to Deepa, she braced herself for potential dismissal. To her pleasant surprise, Deepa agreed without a second thought, trusting Pranati's suggestion wholeheartedly. Deepa's willingness to consider Pranati's preferences made her feel valued and respected, a feeling she rarely experienced during similar outings with her mother. As the shop arrived, Girish said: "So, ladies, please get down from the chariot and grace the stores. In the meantime, I will go to the bookstore to pick some books and join you back".

As they walked into Queen's Choice, Pranati felt a surge of gratitude and appreciation for Deepa's open-mindedness and inclusive attitude. At the store, Deepa and Laya wholeheartedly appreciated Pranati's selections, admiring her sense of style and how thoughtfully she picked out options that would suit Laya. Queen's Choice, a beautifully handcrafted saree shop on Bridal Street, exuded richness, elegance, and grandeur. Stepping inside felt like entering a treasure trove of tradition and artistry, where every saree told a story of meticulous craftsmanship and cultural heritage. The walls were adorned with vibrant, intricate designs, and the air was filled with the soft rustle of luxurious fabrics. The shop boasted an impressive collection of designer sarees, each one a masterpiece reflecting the richness of Indian culture. Deepa, Pranati, and Laya found themselves deeply connected to their roots as they explored the exquisite array of sarees, appreciating both the quality of the materials and the refined aesthetics. Queen's Choice seamlessly blended traditional charm with contemporary style, offering a perfect blend of stuff and style that left them in awe and enriched their shopping experience.

In the midst of this, Sudha called Pranati, advising her not to get carried away and to avoid intruding on her in-laws' affairs. This left Pranati in a dilemma, unsure whether to pull back as her mother suggested or to continue bonding with her mother-in-law and sister-in-law. Conflicted but determined to follow her heart, Pranati decided to enjoy the shopping experience with Deepa and Laya, immersing herself in the moment. Girish joined them. He saw the saree that Pranati selected for Laya and said, "It is beautiful! Where is Pranati's saree?"

After they finished selecting a saree for Laya, Girish and Deepa urged Pranati to choose one for herself. Pranati hesitated, mentioning that she already had plenty of sarees from her wedding. Just then, the shopkeeper asked if the saree was also for their daughter. Girish, with a warm smile, gently pulled Pranati to his side, patted her back, and said, "It is for this daughter of ours." Pranati was deeply touched and overjoyed. At that moment, she felt her heart break through the thorny fences created by her mind. The gesture of unconditional love from her in-laws meant more to her than the six yards of saree. Overwhelmed with gratitude, she stood still, her eyes filling with tears, feeling truly accepted and cherished in her new family. This experience was not just about shopping; it symbolized a deeper connection and acceptance, something Pranati had longed for, making the shopping trip a memorable and cherished moment in Pranati's life.

Sudha was relenting a bit as she did not hear many complaints about Pranati's in-laws. She would bring up the past with Sudhir when she was upset, and during one of the rants, she said she was hoping Pranati and Shreyas would not end up being like them. Sudhir sighed, "Thank God, one size does not fit all. Her life is not the same as yours, and people in her life are different. Why spew your bitterness into her head and heart? Let her learn her life's lessons. Sudha, for heaven's sake, please do not see today with yesterday's lens." For a moment, Sudha felt what Sudhir said was true.

Pranati gradually realized that her in-laws were genuinely kind and caring people, a stark contrast to the negative image her mother had painted. Sudha's opinions had been heavily influenced by her own difficult experiences, leading her to caution Pranati against potential troubles. However, as Pranati spent more time with Deepa and Girish, she saw their sincere efforts to include her and make her feel loved. This prompted Pranati to introspect deeply, recognizing that her mother's fears were rooted in her unique past and didn't necessarily apply to her situation. She came to understand that one size doesn't fit all, and each family dynamic is distinct. Embracing this realization, Pranati felt grateful for her in-laws' warmth and decided to trust her own experiences rather than relying solely on her mother's biases.

5. Base for Decisions

"Sometimes you make the right decision.
Sometimes you make the decision right."

– Phillip C McGraw

One fine Sunday afternoon, Pranati was resting after a heavy meal when she got a call from her dear friend Priya. Pranati smiled as she remembered her firebrand friend who always had something to rebel about. Priya was a good debater in college and had the knack of logically bringing out points that made the opponents bite the dust very soon in a debate. Pranati and Priya had lost touch over the years, and the phone call was a pleasant surprise. Pranati greeted her friend warmly, enquired about her parents and siblings, and was moving on to speak about her spouse when Priya cut her off abruptly and asked her to meet her for an evening stroll.

Priya was nearby, and they decided to meet up in a nearby park. Pranati walked in early, and her hands were already restless, wanting to give a warm hug to Priya. A few minutes later, when Priya walked up, Pranati's enthusiasm gave way to deep concern. What had happened to Priya's smile? Why was her face so drawn and her gait without any energy? Instead of walking, Pranati wanted to listen with attention, and they both found a seat in a quiet corner. Pranati was beside herself and popped the questions as soon as they sat. Where was she working? Were there any issues at the office? When did she marry? Priya gave a wry smile and began her story.

After college, she got a nice placement in a good company. Priya had climbed up year after year in her career. Her go-getter attitude had made her the favorite of her managers. She was smart enough to ask for the raise she deserved and was financially well-placed in a few years. Her family was asking her to get married, and she was skeptical about marriage. She was fiercely independent and did not want to make any compromises. Even caring advice from others was not welcome in her world. She had decided that she was not marriage-ready. Though she loved children, her childhood was not great, and she was not sure about her parenting skills. The idea of going with an arranged match did not appeal to her. A self-made woman can find her match. She had met her husband, Preetham in the office. He was a pleasant person, skilled at work and socially.

Pranati was shocked to know that Priya had opted for a love marriage! Pranati said, "Priya, with your adamant, overly logical, and stubborn nature, I can't believe you could fall in love!" Priya said, "Yes, Pranati, now if I turn back, even I am surprised, how could I not see what I was getting into! Initially, I had kept a distance from Preetham, who is a soft-spoken and socially adept colleague. However, as we collaborated on projects, I began to notice the subtle yet significant ways he impacted me. One day, during a heated discussion, Preetham diffused the tension with a calm, thoughtful response that acknowledged my logic while gently offering an alternative perspective. This moment, where I felt I was truly understood, sparked a change in me, Pranati".

Pranati noticed that as and when Priya was talking about Preetham, she was blushing, and her love for Preetham was evident in her eyes. Pranati was also engrossed in listening to Priya. Priya recalled one more instance, "Another instance I want to tell you, Pranati, during a team lunch, I was charmed by Preetham's genuine interest in everyone's stories, including mine. His attentiveness and gentle humor created an atmosphere where I felt comfortable and appreciated." Pranati felt this was quite contrasting with Priya's usual guardedness.

Priya went on, "One evening, as we were working together on a tight deadline, I experienced a quiet, shared moment with Preetham. Amidst the stress, he handed over a cup of coffee just the way I love coffee! You know he remembered my preferences. This small act of kindness, without any expectation, touched me deeply. The most unforgettable moment of my life was during an office celebration when Preetham invited me to dance!"

Pranati gave a shocked look! "Priya, you and dance? You have two left legs in dance. I remember, in school, because of the art teachers' pressure, I had to include you in dance, and it was a nightmare for me to teach you dance, and I remember how you had cursed the art of dancing!" Priya smiled and continued, "Initially, I was, but I found myself enjoying the dance, captivated by his graceful movements and the easy, encouraging way he leads. It's in these moments—when Preetham's actions consistently showed respect, understanding, and kindness—that my defenses slowly crumbled. I realized my feelings for him had grown into love, and I embraced them without questioning, drawn irresistibly to the warmth and stability he brought into my life. Over time, our frequency of coffee breaks, lunches, and dinners increased. I learned that Preetham was the first child and had two younger brothers. He mentioned that his father was a government employee but had gambling issues, and the family had debts to repay. His mother, though working, enabled his father by giving him a share of her salary as well. He had studied hard and had gotten this job. He was earning the most and contributed to clearing the debts. His brothers were still studying, and he had responsibilities to shoulder. I noticed that he was interested in me, but his commitments were stopping him from popping the question."

Pranati was curious to know more. She said, "Priya, I am very curious to know how you abandoned your logic, how you got blinded by love, and how you proposed to Preetham?". Priya said, "It was not me, he proposed," and as she said, Pranati noticed the most feminine grace and beauty in Priya's eyes, which she had never witnessed before. Pranati started teasing Priya and said, "Now do not censor anything, tell me how it happened?" Pranati showed her interest in her gleaming eyes.

Priya continued, "We had an office outing at a picturesque lakeside resort, and the team decided to spend the evening around a bonfire. As the night progressed, laughter and music filled the air. Preetham, knowing my love for quiet moments and scenic beauty, suggested we take a walk by the lake. I agreed, appreciating the chance to escape the crowd for a while. Walking along the moonlit path, we chatted about our work, shared experiences, and dreams. Preetham, sensing the perfect moment, paused by a secluded spot. I still can't forget the way the moonlight was shimmering on the water. He took a deep breath, his heart racing, and turned to me with a soft smile. "Priya," he began, his voice gentle but steady, "there's something I've been wanting to tell you for a while now." I was curious but calm, and looked into his eyes, sensing the seriousness of the moment. He continued,

"I know you're logical and stubborn," he continued, "and I admire that about you. But I've come to see that beneath that, you have a heart that's kind and passionate. You challenge me, inspire me, and make me want to be better every day." He took my hand in his, and for the first time, I didn't pull away, feeling a warmth spread through me.

"Being with you has shown me what it means to truly connect with someone. I've fallen in love with you, Priya. I want to share my life with you, not just as colleagues or friends, but as partners. Will you be with me?" I was taken aback by his heartfelt confession; my usual defenses melted away. I saw the sincerity in his eyes, the genuine love and hope, and realized I felt the same. I replied, "Yes, Preetham. I will." As we embraced under the starlit sky, the lake reflecting our happiness, we both knew this was the start of our beautiful journey together." Pranati was lost in Priya's fairy tale. Suddenly it flashed to Pranati that unlike regular fairy tales, this doesn't sound like the prince and princess married and stayed happily ever after. Pranati broke the silence "Priya that was some romantic story. But now why are you sounding unhappy?" Priya said, "How I wish that moment froze. Life had something else in store Pranati, Soon, we both informed our marriage decision to our families. My family was highly critical and wanted to check his background. Preetham's family was interested in how much I was earning. My parents took all the relatives to meet his family. When they came back, each one had noticed something or other. One aunt was not comfortable with his father's words. They were too phony. The other aunt thought his mother was too sweet, and not real. My mother was not happy about them not having their own home and Preetham shouldering the responsibility of clearing debts. My father was concerned that Preetham was the scapegoat and he had not realized the same. He was paying the price for the irresponsibility of his parents. Preetham has been idealized in his family as someone who will solve all their issues.

I had always thought that my family was over-critical. I have heard enough criticism as a child and am very sensitive to criticism even as an adult. That has forced me to be a perfectionist and has helped me rise in my career. This quality is my strength as well as weakness, Pranati. But the same nature made me go ahead without thinking. Whatever I did, I was convinced that my family would criticize me. Pranati, after we came back from Preetham's house that day when my father first saw him and spoke to Preetham, he warned me. He is a shrewd and pragmatic man who has always been deeply concerned about my well-being and future. I was a fool not to acknowledge him. My dad observed a casual conversation where Preetham mentioned that he doesn't care much for money and prefers to focus on living a fulfilling life. This statement raised a red flag for my dad, who values financial stability and responsibility. After dinner, my dad asked me to join him for a private conversation in his study. With a serious expression, he said, "Priya, there's something important we need to discuss." Sensing my father's concern, I asked, "What is it, Dad?"

He took a deep breath, choosing his words carefully. "I like Preetham; he seems like a good man with a kind heart. But I couldn't help but notice his comment about not caring for money. While it's admirable to focus on living a fulfilling life, financial stability is crucial, especially when considering a future together." I listened attentively, but as usual, I was fuming inside that again my dad was criticizing my choice. Dad said, "Managing finances is an essential part of life. It's not just about having enough money, but about being responsible and planning for the future. I'm worried that Preetham's attitude towards money might lead to difficulties down the road. I want you to think about this seriously." Tears welled up in Priya's eyes." If only I had seen the care and concern in my parents and relatives' feedback! They were trying to ensure that I was peaceful in my new home. They are all my well-wishers. Maybe they did not know how to communicate, and I was not good at comprehending what they conveyed".

We got married in a temple as I did not want to splurge on the ceremony, and I don't have a belief in the rituals. The wedding was a simple affair, and I decided I would never discuss my marital problems with my parents. After all, it was my choice, and my ego was not ready to accept that I could be wrong in any way. Preetham was regularly clearing debts, and to run the house, he was relying on my salary. We decided not to think of a child till the debts were cleared. Both of us had opportunities to go abroad. We traveled on onsite assignments and every dollar we earned was given to clear the debts.

My father was concerned more and more as he saw his son-in-law not rising to his new role as husband. My father always used to think aloud with my mom, "Did he not want a home of his own where he could raise his children in safety and security? What was the role of his daughter? Only an ATM to clear someone's loan. What happens to her desires? Should they be shelved forever?" His experience with gamblers made him see the dark abyss his child would fall into. No gambler's debts have ever been cleared. My mother wanted to see her grandchild. She had her arguments. "Was not the purpose of marriage securing the future of children? Who will marry to clear the debts, except maybe her rebel of a daughter?" She had struggled with raising me. As a child, it seems I was sensitive. My mother would tell all the time that overthinking was my second nature. I was used to holding grudges, and my mother's efforts to eliminate this nature had not borne fruit. My story in my head was real for me, and in my mind, my parents and caring relatives were assigned the role of villains."

Priya continued, "I was hoping that my in-laws were not so critical. They were not even interested in me as a human being. Preetham was completely raised on the story that his mother was a victim and was sacrificing her all to raise her children. The reality was that she and my father-in-law were jointly causing the financial mess. With no qualms, they ask Preetham for money. Preetham does not dare to say no as he does not want to face his mother's emotional tantrums. I have stopped talking to my father-in-law and have banned him from coming home. My mother-in-law has made me the witch in her family circle for questioning their irresponsibility and saying no to their irrational money demands. Preetham is also very image-conscious and gullible to praise. Any money request from his fleecing relatives, he uses my name instead of refusing himself. Preetham is upset that I use a harsh tone with his mother, whom he has put on a pedestal. This has been a constant source of fighting in our marriage. I am tired, Pranati. I am seriously thinking of getting out of this marriage itself."

Pranati had learned over the years that there are always two sides to the story. She could not digest the two contrasting episodes of Joyful Romance and the romantic hero turning villain! Pranati told Priya," Don't jump the gun, Priya. These are not decisions to be taken in haste. You know, Shreyas' Grandma Sumathi, my favorite granny, is an amazing mentor and super friendly. She is the reason I got adjusted to my new home after marriage. Priya, please, I want you both to come home and meet her once. Please don't say no. Granny always reiterates this point; Do not make decisions when you are emotionally unstable." Pranati's heart went out to Priya. She was so desperate that she wished to just pick a magic wand and set her life right. Pranati invited Priya and Preetham to her home. She wanted her friend to have a fun time and a break from extended family issues.

Pranati was sharing Priya's story with Shreyas who silently listened. Shreyas made a strong comment, "Bringing up the children in the right way and inculcating values is so important!" Pranati said, "You mean Priya's parents haven't raised them properly? What are you saying? As adults, it is an individual decision and choice in marriage, right?" Shreyas cut the conversation with a lighter note and teased Pranati by holding her hand and looking into her eyes," Your honor, it was my opinion, not a verdict! For Preetham's faults, do not penalize me!" Both burst out into laughter.

On a relaxed Sunday morning at Shreyas' house, the air was filled with the melodious tunes of Vividh Bharati, setting a nostalgic backdrop for the day. The living room was warm and inviting, bathed in soft sunlight streaming through the windows. Shreyas and Pranati, his parents, and his grandparents gathered at the dining table, creating a lively and intimate atmosphere.

The rich aroma of freshly brewed chai, mingled with the scent of homemade snacks, adds to the cozy ambiance. Sumathi was in her rocking chair, leaning back in her armchair, a contented smile on her face as she tapped her foot to an old Bollywood classic. "This song always brings back memories," she mused, her eyes twinkling. Pranati, curious, asked, "Ajji, will you tell us about your romance with Ajja? We've heard bits and pieces, but we'd love to hear the full story."

Sumathi chuckled, "Oh, those were different times," she began, her voice warm with nostalgia. "We met in a local fair, you know, the kind where everyone from the village gathered. I was there with my friends, and your Ajja saw me at a stall, bargaining fiercely over some bangles. It seems he was struck by my confidence and my laughter. He used to say I had the most infectious laugh. He kept following me around the fair, trying to muster up the courage to talk to me. Finally, he bought a string of jasmine flowers and awkwardly handed it to me. It was the sweetest gesture." Shreyas and Pranati listened, enthralled, as Sumathi continued, "Our families knew each other, so it wasn't long before we started meeting more often. Our courtship was filled with stolen glances, secret notes, and the occasional chaperoned walk. We didn't have the freedom or the technology you youngsters have today. Every moment together was precious and fleeting. We had to make the most of it." As the playlist transitioned to another timeless melody, Sumathi smiled wistfully. "This song," she said softly, "was playing the night he proposed. We were at a family gathering, and he somehow convinced my brother to let us sneak away for a few minutes. Under the moonlit sky, by the river, he asked me to be his forever." Shreyas, holding Pranati's hand, felt a surge of affection and respect for his grandparents. "You two are an inspiration," he said warmly. "Your love story is beautiful." Pranati nodded, her eyes shining. "It's amazing how love transcends time. Your story feels like a movie." Immediately, the scene shifted as they heard the calling bell buzzing. It was Priya and Preetham who were on the verge of breaking their relationship! Before they arrived, Pranati whom Shreyas called "chatterbox with a sieve mouth," had given a detailed open narration to the whole family. Sumathi was quietly watching the two. Pranati had asked her to guide her on how to help her friend.

Preetham and Priya felt solace and a temporary escape from their troubles. As they stepped inside, they were enveloped by the warmth and affection. The house radiated an aura of love and togetherness, with laughter and affectionate conversations filling the air. Shreyas' parents shared stories of their struggles and triumphs, subtly reminding Preetham and Priya of the resilience required in a marriage. Sumathi provided a living testament to enduring love and explained the challenges in her marriage, offering a glimpse of what a lifelong partnership can look like. They spoke candidly about their challenges, emphasizing the importance of patience and understanding. The day progressed, and Preetham and Priya found themselves relaxing, their tensions easing in the nurturing environment. The loving interactions between family members created a sense of peace and security, making them realize their relationship's potential for growth and healing.

When it was time to leave, they felt renewed hope and determination to work through their issues, inspired by the love and harmony that vibrated throughout Pranati's home. They both bowed to Sumathi traditionally as a mark of respect. Sumathi blessed them," Let each day of your life be as beautiful as the day you fell in love." That blessing was an eye-opener for the couple. Sumathi said, "You are also like Pranati to me, please keep coming." Priya melted in the warmth of Sumathi's affection. Pranati was bidding bye to Priya and by that time, Preetham opened the car door for Priya. Priya was surprised for a moment. She had seen this gesture when he proposed to her. After that, she lost her friend to family toxicity. It was nice to get that friend in him back again. Pranati and Shreyas observed that and exchanged happy smiles. Priya smiled and sat gently next to Preetham. The experience of talking to thoughtful elders at Pranati's house prompted them to rethink their decision to break their marriage, recognizing that with effort and commitment, they too can create a home filled with love.

After they left, Sumathi started, "The couple is fine, and it looks like a normal misunderstanding". Sumathi was thinking for a while and said she saw two deluded individuals who had no clue about marriage. "One is deluded by her ego's story of independence and perfection. The other has delusions about his image in his family and his weakness for praise. Priya thought she could handle it all. Preetham was blind and could not see how his family was fleecing him. He was enabling a bunch of freeloaders." Everyone was surprised. Sumathi asked Pranathi to find out what they thought about marriage.

When Pranati asked her friend, she said she had not thought much about marriage. She was attracted to Preetham, and marriage was the logical culmination point for the relationship. For Preetham, it was a simple convenience to close his parents' debts sooner as Priya was working. He would argue that he had mentioned this before marriage, and Priya had married him with eyes fully open. Pranati was herself lost with such intent for marriage. Both of them had their agenda. They had not thought of building a loving home with giggling children. Money, ego, fake grandiose image, and a misconception about loyalty to family ties, even when they are clearly on the wrong path, were about to ruin their marriage.

Sumathi saw two adult-looking children when she met them next. She started chatting with Priya. Over time, Priya opened up to a friendly grandmother. Sumathi asked her to step back and let Preetham handle his family. Because of her mistrust, she would watch every step that Preetham took as far as his family was concerned. She wanted to know every small detail. Preetham had started hiding things from her to avoid conflicts. An anxious Priya was unwilling to let go of her control. Sumathi told her to try it for a month and report the results.

Over time, Priya's smile got broader. The results were far better than what she expected. Initially, she was very reluctant. The first time she stopped asking Preetham about what he does when a money demand arises, she had butterflies in her stomach. She listened to a conversation where he used her name and said no. Preetham was puzzled that she did not raise the topic and argue. She stopped arguing with his mother and even stopped talking to her over the phone. She told Preetham she would not interfere. Preetham was by nature a cautious person when it came to money. But his image was bigger. And he had no intention of losing the fake image any time soon.

He had no option but to start saying no, where it mattered. She heard him take his youngest brother to task. As she pulled back and observed, she saw where she was going wrong. She did not have to react to everything. Her mother-in-law used her reaction to build the next set of false stories. She stopped explaining herself too much to Preetham. Earlier, she would have said something harsh in a rage and would spend days pacifying him. She started taking over her home as a true Grihini. She was making decisions on the home front. Her home started getting her warmth and love. She realized she was the pillar of love and strength for her home.

Quietly, she started building her connection with other relatives in the family. Not all of them were her mother-in-law. Many understood her part and even saw why she had to make the decisions she took. As her friend circle increased, her influence started growing quietly. A silent revolution had begun. Preetham's parents were getting isolated as the reality started emerging. Priya could hardly believe her ears when Preetham's maternal uncle openly said that her in-laws were troubling their adult children. Their irresponsibility had made one of their sons go wayward. As people questioned her mother-in-law's narrative openly, she began to keep her financial deals to herself. Too much was getting exposed. She had lost the trust of most of her family.

Preetham was seeing the disconnect between him and Priya. He was not fully ready to accept his mistakes. But he stopped criticizing Priya. He was not getting the reaction when he triggered her. She had learned to be neutral. A pensive Preetham was learning hard to reflect. His ego would not let go so easily. He was the eternal victim just like his parents. He had to break this along with wrong notions that the world owed him because he suffered.

Sumathi was happy with the changes in the couple. They were both reflecting on their marriage. As Girish noted, their issues had nothing to do with marriage. Everywhere they would face the same problems because they were not willing to reflect, question, seek guidance, take accountability for their thoughts and actions as adults, learn, and shift gears. Yes, they both had troubled childhoods. But as adults, they were powerful enough to reparent themselves and heal the trauma. Why restrict oneself and be a Bonsai? We were made to spread roots far and wide. Blaming parents or childhood forever was not going to keep them happy. There is an easy way to learn, from experienced, wise people. And the hard way of experiencing, heartache, anger, ill health. Pranati's heart sang as she saw her friend and her spouse choose the easy way. They would be fine.

As she looked at Shreyas, a small question arose. Did they marry for the right reasons? What would keep them together when things got rough? Was the heady feeling of love enough to sustain the onslaught of daily stress and strain?

6. Deal of a Marriage

After a month of marriage, Shreyas resumed his office. He had already gotten a placement in India while wrapping up a project in London. Pranati was yet to report to her new office this coming month. She decided to take up her office a bit late so she could settle down in her new home after marriage. She was sipping her morning tea on a rocking chair when she received a call from Shreyas. Shreyas told her over the phone, "Pranati, today, my boss Nikhil has called us for dinner at his residence. I will be back from work and pick you up by 7 in the evening.". Sumathi was making wicks for the brass lamps, sitting near the pooja room, and listening to her favorite devotional songs. She teased

Pranati, "I can see you turning pink when your husband calls you, even if you knew each other before marriage! That's why they say marriages are made in heaven." Pranati gave a blushing smile. Sumathi continued, "Pranati, what will you wear for the evening? Dress up nicely and go. Wear your nice gold bangles, chain, and saree." Pranati gave a weird look and said, "Ajji, I am not going to any wedding. I don't like dressing up too much for casual visits." Sumathi said, "Dressing up will attract positivity. It is not to show off. It is very scientific that wearing noble metals like gold or silver at pressure points of the ears, neck, and hand will keep a woman's health and spirit in great shape. Unfortunately, young girls think it is a matter of likes, dislikes, or convenience. Dressing up will invoke the inner essence in women." Pranati had never heard something like this. She was awe-struck at Sumathi's wisdom. Sumathi said, "Anyway, on some other day, I will talk about this leisurely. Now I need to go to the temple." Pranati went to her room and took out her beautiful saree. Unusual for herself, she decided to wear nice jewelry after listening to Sumathi.

She then came down to give tea to her father-in-law. She was searching for him when Deepa called out, "Your father-in-law will be in the garden with his green children. Look for him there." Girish was a passionate gardener. Post-retirement, he had tended to his garden and was taking care of plants like his own children. His wife enjoyed his childlike enthusiasm when he would pull her out to show her a vibrant flower or a small bird's nest. The rest of the time, he had taken over household regular shopping, walking with a small group of close friends, pranayama, and scriptural study. He was sitting under the neem tree and was reading a book by his Guru when he was interrupted by Pranati and the aroma of tea. Pranati gave the teacup to Girish, and the book in his hand caught her attention. "Appa, I see many of this person's books in our house. Who is he?" Girish told his new daughter-in-law about his Guru with deep reverence and admiration. "Pranati, I regard him as a stalwart. He is a remarkable figure, a Sanskrit scholar with a PhD in quantum science who has seamlessly blended science and spirituality. My Guru's role as an accomplished teacher and a strict disciplinarian who firmly believes in self-introspection and personal accountability has profoundly impacted my life. He has guided me on the path of wisdom, discipline, and inner peace, ultimately shaping me into a better individual. I am fortunate to have such a guru. I connect deeply with him."

Taking responsibility for oneself—that one quality—made Girish a trustworthy, reliable person whom family and friends looked up to for advice in times of trouble. His professional growth had reiterated this point again and again. He was a legend in his domain but was deeply respected by his colleagues, seniors, and juniors for his integrity. He had developed the uncanny ability to be fair and listen to all sides with his head and heart. Young and old alike basked in his wise company and anecdotes. He would not directly say what to do or how anyone's behavior had caused the problem in the first place. His scriptural background allowed him to set the right context and nudge people to introspect. They would resist his ideas, but ultimately they realized their responsibility. He had noticed that Pranati was getting comfortable in her home and sometimes felt free to seek his counsel.

.Pranati asked Girish, taking lenience, "Appa, don't get me wrong if I ask you something. How could you manage both in-laws and parents in one home? I mean, it is so difficult!" Girish smiled and said, "Yes, it was not an easy ride. Since both Deepa and I were hard-core professionals, as a family, we all sat down and took a call after Shreyas was born, that even Deepa's parents would move in here. Earlier, they were staying in Mysuru. Deepa was getting stressed as it was difficult to visit them regularly. Initially, it was planned more for professional convenience. But later, we felt fortunate to have blessings and love from both sides. But it was sometimes a bumpy ride. Decisions would go wrong. Sometimes, the ego is big, and it is hard for many, especially elders, to accept it quickly and take the necessary corrective steps. They would give all sorts of explanations, except for accepting their part. Being with two sets of elders at home has taught me to be gentle but firm. I wanted to raise my children with the values I was privileged to get from my parents, but times have changed. I hold myself responsible when my children err and have tried to guide them as much as possible. I am no longer sure what values they have picked up from family and outside influences."

As he was thinking about his parenting pluses and minuses, Shreyas joined them. He said, "Appa, Pranati, and I are going out for dinner to my manager's place. Amma and Ajji are not home. Please tell them not to cook for us." Pranati said, "I already informed them. But how come you are back home so early?". Shreyas said, "I thought of taking some calls from home, freshening up, and then going to Nikhil's place." Jovially, Girish asked about Nikhil, "So Shreyas, how is your official father-in-law?" Shreyas replied, "Nikhil is an amazing gentleman. He supports the team fully. We feel safe to take risks after discussing them with him, and he covers our dark spots where needed. He treats everyone with respect." Girish felt happy that his son was not stressed at work.

Shreyas and Pranati, newlyweds and brimming with excitement, dressed up traditionally for that special evening. Shreyas donned a crisp kurta-pajama, while Pranati looked stunning in her elegant saree, complete with traditional jewelry and delicate makeup. As they stepped out, Shreyas felt a surge of pride and joy. He drove his car, whistling a happy tune and glancing occasionally at his beautiful wife beside him. The journey to his boss's house for dinner was filled with anticipation and a sense of shared accomplishment, as Shreyas was eager to introduce Pranati and showcase their grace and charm as a couple.

Pranati and Shreyas stepped into Nikhil's house. Nikhil opened the door and invited them inside. The living room was tastefully decorated, and the most striking feature was a large, blown-up picture of Nikhil and his wife hanging prominently on the wall. Pranati's eyes widened in shock as she took in the image. Her breath caught as she recognized Neelima, her role model from her school days. Neelima was quite an inspiration to Pranati, having been a top model admired by many young girls. Page three gossip that Pranati had keenly followed would invariably have some glam and glitter about Neelima. She was involved in multiple scandals and a divorce. She had married the most popular hero of her time when her career had peaked. He had turned out to be an arrogant, self-absorbed person who valued her only until she had projects lined up. He had cheated on her, and she had walked out with huge alimony.

Pranati was curious to hear the rest of Neelima's life story. Lots of questions were springing up in Pranati's mind. She was staring at the picture when Nikhil explained, "I met my charming woman while she was extensively traveling, and so was I. Marriages are made in heaven. For both of us, we got the second opportunity to feel heaven! Please come in; I will fill in the details of our story later." Just then, Neelima entered the living room. She was dressed elegantly in a simple yet sophisticated cotton salwar kameez. Her presence was graceful and poised, reflecting the charm and elegance she was known for during her modeling days. Neelima smiled warmly and walked towards Pranati and Shreyas. Pranati was even more awestruck to see Neelima in person, recalling how she adored her during her school years. Neelima greeted them with a gentle nod and said, "Welcome to our home. Please come inside and make yourselves comfortable." Her voice was kind, adding to the inviting atmosphere. Pranati felt a mix of emotions—excitement, nostalgia, and a touch of disbelief—at meeting her idol in such an unexpected context. She smiled, trying to contain her excitement as she and Shreyas followed Neelima further into the house.

They all sat on the sofa, and the cook served the starter drink and tasty snacks. The conversation flowed, and Nikhil said, "So, Pranati, nice to see you and Shreyas together. As a well-wisher, I want to tell you something. Keep the love alive and reduce your expectations in married life." He exchanged a smile with Neelima. Shreyas asked, "You both got married very late, right?" Nikhil continued, "Oh, that's a long story. Shreyas, I was raised in a traditional family and was attracted to a career woman in my twenties. My father had warned me about the girl's ambitions not matching my ideas of a spouse. But I was a typical young man without enough experience to consider what mattered to me. I was blinded by double income and quick material success, so I went ahead with the marriage. It was a disaster from day one, as our values clashed. My ex-wife saw any work at home as compromising her career. I was ambitious and did not want to spend even a second extra on home maintenance. She had a weird idea that marriage meant chores were split 50-50. Our marriage deal included 50-50 chores; she would pay for the home expenses, and I would work on a loan for our new home. Love was not there to begin with. A marriage of convenience, the deal fell apart within a year. We parted ways. I was depressed, decided to give up everything, and started to travel intensely to compose myself.

I still remember that evening in a London café. I entered the cafe, shaking off the evening chill. I spotted an empty table near the window, sat down with my book, and ordered a coffee. As I waited, my gaze landed on a familiar face: Neelima, my classmate, seated a few tables away, absorbed in her thoughts. After a slight hesitation, I walked over and asked, "Neelima, is that you?" She looked up, surprised, but then broke into a warm smile. "Yes!" I reminded her of our school days and introduced myself again as an adult. I was a huge fan of hers. I gestured to the empty chair and asked, "May I join you?" "Of course," she replied, her eyes lighting up. We settled in, and the conversation moved easily as we caught up on our lives, sharing the ups and downs we had experienced. I spoke about my work and how I was adjusting to life post-divorce, while Neelima shared her journey from modeling to finding a new purpose in life after her divorce. Our initial polite conversation deepened as we found common ground in our shared experiences, discussing our struggles, the lessons we had learned, and how we were trying to grow from them all. A mutual understanding and respect began to form, bridging the gap between our past and present selves. As the evening wore on, we realized the cafe was starting to empty, but we did not want the conversation to end. We laughed over anecdotes, finding comfort and joy in each other's company. I looked at Neelima with newfound admiration and said, "You know, I never expected to find someone who understands this part of my life so well." Neelima nodded, her smile soft and genuine. "Neither did I. It feels like we were meant to connect." We exchanged contact information, feeling a sense of anticipation and hope. As we stepped out of the cafe together, the evening air was warm, and we walked side by side, knowing this was the start of something special. We met when we were much older and were tired of material excess. We wanted peace and a quiet home."

The conversation veered towards the ex-wife and ex-husband. Nikhil and Neelima spoke about the issues with the ex-wife and ex-husband. Pranati felt that the narrative was one-sided. Shreyas had almost put Nikhil and Neelima in the victim slot and was very sympathetic. Pranati had her doubts. A story has multiple shades. Something was amiss. After dinner, Shreyas and Pranati took leave from Nikhil's house. As they drove back, Pranati said, "Something is fishy, Shreyas. I need to know the other side of the stories about their ex-partners so a fair conclusion can be drawn." Shreyas was adamant that his boss and his wife were angels without wings, and it was obvious the other party had abused them.

The next morning, after Shreyas left for the office, Girish and Pranati went grocery shopping. Pranati told him she was confused about a point and wanted his opinion. Girish stopped for coffee on their way back, and Pranati narrated the previous day's episode about Nikhil and Neelima. She told her point, "Appa, I feel that in a marriage, both partners are equally involved in the success or failure." Girish acknowledged, "Yes, Pranati, you are right. Material truth is always relative, and there will be as many shades as people. This is not gossip. It's a thought-provoking case study on the concept of marriage. Let us continue this discussion once Shreyas gets back home."

That day, after dinner, Pranati raised the topic of the previous day's dinner scene. Shreyas was flipping the channels on TV and said, "Past tense queen, are you still stuck there? By the way, why are you so concerned? You like gossip, don't you? It's their life. They are adults, and they will decide for their lives." Girish interrupted, "Shreyas, she is not gossiping. She is trying to get her doubts clarified on fundamental issues. Now, Shreyas and Pranati, think of two things. Knowing Nikhil is ambitious, would he marry Neelima if he was not a divorcee and she did not have a fat alimony? Neelima is used to a very different world than Nikhil. Maybe she wants kids and is tired of two-timing men in her field. She may want stability and was ok with marrying Nikhil. She looks like she is well-adjusted as a homemaker. What happens when Nikhil starts showing his true colours?"

Pranati found herself thinking about Girish's questions. She was wondering why it bothered her so much. She had met them only once. They seemed genuine. They were warmly welcomed. But her instincts told her something was off. Girish had not answered straight. He had made her think about the instance.

Pranati did not have a solid answer. Girish asked Shreyas to ponder as well.

Shreyas started, "Appa, I know Nikhil as a colleague and manager. Personal story, I am not interested. It is their private life. Divorces are common these days. They seem to have a genuine reason to part ways. They can do what they want." Girish was shocked by his son's reaction. He was thinking, Would Shreyas have the same answer if anything challenging happened in his marriage?

Pranati was emotional, as she valued marriage and was working on laying the foundation for her warm home. She had seen her mother's detachment in the name of independence and how it had made her and her brother very guarded. Her mother would laugh at anything emotional about the home. For her, it was a convenient shelter. Pranati was opening up now, liking the atmosphere in her home and the caring, sharing, and concern for other family members. She did not want to miss something precious, subtle, and crucial for the human spirit. She was disappointed that Shreyas did not endorse her views.

Shreyas continued, "For them, marriage is for partnership. The partnership includes sharing all resources. Money or home—a long partnership with the right person builds family resources. Even the wrong person gets alimony. They will have enough to enjoy life and retire rich." Girish could hold himself no longer. He cut in, "Shreyas, what about the other needs? Need for a warm home to come back to, need for affection, need for stability, raising good children, and sharing resources wisely. What about responsibility as a man? Is it not a man's role to provide for his family and secure their future? Without such structure and personal responsibility, society will crumble."

Deepa heard the raised voices and came out to check. Shreyas was saying, "Appa, that was in your time. Today, we live in a world where all boundaries are blurred. When women are working and willing to share the bill, what is the need to stick to the old structure? With such a huge population, why have kids and add to the misery? Legally, we have to be married to secure material resources. That's it." Deepa was surprised and asked, "Why marry for just that? If you do not want to raise children, marriage is irrelevant." She was in tears when she said, "I was dreaming of grandchildren."

Shreyas was exasperated and said, "Amma, I have not thought about children. Neither has Pranati. At present, we are focusing on our careers. We were discussing about Nikhil, and I was stating their point of view. Not that we don't want children forever." Shreyas was getting confused. He was raised with good values. He had grown up in the warm company of his grandparents and under the protective guidance of his father. He valued Deepa's kind and firm discipline, the sibling banter with Laya, and his friendship with Pranati. Did he not want a similar home for the next generation? But Nikhil seemed to have it all. He decided to drop the issue for now. Pranati went in quietly. They had not thought of children for now, yes. But she loved children, and Shreyas knew that.

Girish consoled Deepa, saying that Shreyas and Pranati may need some time. Internally, his mind was in huge conflict. He was convinced by what the scriptures said: the family phase of life (Grihastha ashrama) was not just a convenient union for two people; it was for the safety and security of the next generation. Raising children with good values is the foundation of a healthy society. We contribute to a healthy society by raising children with the right values. Have we not taken so much from society, both material and subtle? So many thoughts rose in his mind. "The circumstances of life are different—some thriving, some suffering. Will the same situations continue forever? Of course, not. As karma shifts, good times follow bad times. Is everyone wise enough to know it all? Was his son using an umbrella statement to escape his duties of raising future generations?" He was now blaming himself. He should have had a serious conversation with Shreyas about marriage, a nurturing institution for the next generation. There were duties associated with the roles of husband and father. He had assumed his son understood the shift in roles when he married. He realized this generation needed a lot more open communication. Though it was a bit too late, he decided to make his son understand his roles and responsibilities.

Deepa was winding up her kitchen cleaning when Girish broke the silence coming out of his self-talk.

"Oh my God, I just can't believe this. Deepa, I read a lot about Neelima in newspapers when she was an active model. She was in an open marriage. It was an open secret. I think Shreyas hasn't been told the real story of his boss, Nikhil. Now I can connect the dots. When she got divorced, that open marriage partner was Nikhil." Deepa was cleaning the kitchen when she was talking to Girish. She said, "I'm uncomfortable listening to this concept, Girish. We will feel like bending our heads in shame even to talk about this with our grown-up children. I don't know how they can indulge in such an act!"

Sumathi was reading a book on a rocking chair when she heard the conversation about open marriage. When Deepa offered a glass of milk to Sumathi, which was her routine post-dinner, Sumathi took the glass of milk and asked Deepa, "By the way, Deepa, what is open marriage? Does it mean the invitation is open to all?" Both Girish and Deepa looked at each other and burst out laughing, while Sumathi innocently had a puzzled look on her face and gaped at them.

The coming Saturday, Shreyas was surprised when his father asked him to join him to meet his Guru, Dr. Prakasham. Girish had not insisted on any ritualistic practices for his children. Deepa and Sumathi would insist, and he did not interfere. Shreyas was free and joined him. They paid their respects and sat quietly. As if on cue, he asked about Shreyas' marriage. He responded that it went well. He asked Shreyas to be around. He and Girish got into a deep discussion on an Upanishad. Once done, Girish requested that Dr. Prakasham share his thoughts about marriage for Shreyas' benefit.

Dr. Prakasham smiled at Shreyas and congratulated him on his marriage. He started discussing the institution of marriage from a spiritual angle: "Two people coming together is not a coincidence. The universe conspires to bring souls together so they can give birth to other souls. Life is sacred. Imagine the sanctity of marriage, the foundation for another life form. The husband and wife support each other until the children are grown. For a successful marriage, respect for each other and friendship are the cornerstones. Essentially, setting aside egos helps children grow up in warm homes. I feel sad that today's generation has decided to misinterpret everything beautiful in our culture. There was no competition between men and women until this time. They supported each other through thick and thin, ensuring the future was secure for the next generation. In the traditional context, they never forgot their journey and were adept at self-reflection, expanding into giants of character and strength as they aged. Money as a central theme has become the crucial ingredient for broken homes. Divorce is easy, but when will man learn to hold himself accountable? When will he step up to his role and grow into his true potential?" He asked Shreyas, "Do you think men can live happily without positive emotions?" Shreyas was at a loss for words. A quiet father-son duo walked back home. It was a mind-churning experience for Shreyas.

The next day at the office, Nikhil joined Shreyas for lunch. Shreyas asked Nikhil, "Nikhil, how about your kids? We didn't see them yesterday." The answer was a shocker. Nikhil said, "We do not want children, Shreyas. We both want only a fun life partner and loads of cash to have fun. Children would be a hassle. 18 to 20 years go to waste taking care of them." Shreyas lumped in his throat and kept quiet. Shreyas realized why his father had taken him to Dr. Prakasham. For the first time, Shreyas was thinking about the purpose of life, marital context, and his expanded roles and responsibilities. Earlier, he never had self-doubt. But, now, he was not sure. Would he fill in his father's shoes? He remembered the many times when his father had warned him about his ways and how he was saved from his idiotic decisions. He had attributed all his success to himself. A small tear appeared as he started to see the firm guidance he had gotten from Girish.

Even now, Girish had not failed as a father. He knew his son needed a broader perspective, as he had seen the world. He may have questions that his limited intellect cannot answer. He had taken him to Dr. Prakasham. His heart felt full thinking of his father. He walked in with a lighter heart and asked Girish if he could join him on Saturdays to meet Dr. Prakasham. A surprised Girish nodded and smiled at Pranati. She smiled in return. Girish was at peace that right values would be passed on to coming generations.

7. Mind of a Heart

"True intelligence comes from the mind of the heart,
where love and wisdom unite."

– Unknown

Deepa was preparing to leave for a wedding when she saw Sumathi hold the phone and sit in a daze on a nearby chair. An alarmed Deepa rushed to Sumathi. She handed the phone to Deepa. Tears were streaming down Sumathi's face. Her second daughter, Nalini's husband, Vikram, was hospitalized with a massive heart attack. Girish was not in town. They informed Shreyas and rushed to the hospital to be with Nalini.

Pranati had met Nalini a few times before and after her marriage. Despite being Girish's sister, Nalini seemed less warm and open than him and not as talkative as their mother, Sumathi. Many relatives considered her proud and prudish. Nalini's children were thriving: her elder son was a successful young entrepreneur, and her younger daughter was pursuing a master's degree at a German university. Their family appeared complete and prosperous. Vikram had amassed a fortune in his business and was the welcoming face of their family. Recently, he had embraced spiritual practices, following an internet sensation in the remote Himalayas. Both Vikram's and Nalini's families were carried away with Vikram's influence and presence.

Sumathi sometimes felt that her daughter, Nalini was not as warm as Vikram was towards everyone. She had noticed changes in Nalini over the last few years and initially attributed them to hormonal fluctuations of menopause, hoping she would soon return to her cheerful self. However, this had not happened, and Sumathi worried that something was bothering her. Once, she spoke to Deepa, "Deepa, I've noticed many changes in Nalini. Have you seen it too?" Deepa responded, "Yes, Amma, I have noticed Nalini isn't herself these days. She might be dealing with some family issues and trying to sort things out on her own. Let's give her some time before we speak to her."

Nalini and Deepa cared deeply for each other and were almost the same age, making them more like friends than sisters-in-law. Nalini often confided in Deepa, and they used to discuss every family issue. Their children, who were of similar ages, grew up together. However, as they both became busy raising children and managing their households, their heart-to-heart talks became less frequent.

Shreyas drove Deepa and Sumathi to the hospital. Upon arrival, Nalini's son Nishith escorted them inside, saying, "I need to go out to get some medications and will be back soon. Please wait in the visitor's area." Sumathi looked around for Nalini but didn't see her. She asked, "Nishith, where is Nalini?" Nishith, appearing lost, replied, "Ajji, she didn't want to see Appa in the ICU and is still at home."

Both Sumathi and Deepa were aghast. As they settled into chairs outside the ICU, Sumathi's anger became evident. She couldn't contain herself and said, "How can a wife be so cold? Not being there for her husband during such an emergency? I never raised her to be like this. This is not right! I will call her right away and speak to her." She took out her cell phone. Deepa stopped Sumathi, saying, "No, please don't do that. If Nalini hasn't come here in such an emergency, she must be going through her turmoil. Let's find out later from Nalini. Right now, Vikram's health is the priority."

Vikram underwent a critical stent insertion procedure in the hospital due to a blockage in his heart. The operation was successful, but Vikram was kept under close observation in the ICU for the first two days to monitor his recovery and ensure there were no complications. During this period, the family members were anxious and constantly on edge, praying for his swift recovery. After three days, Vikram's condition stabilized, and he was moved to a regular ward. This transition brought immense relief to the entire family, as it signified a positive turn in his health. The sight of Vikram recovering and seeing that he was getting better by the day brought great comfort and hope to his loved ones. The doctor said he could be discharged in two days.

Shreyas, Deepa, and Sumathi went that Friday morning to take Vikram home from the hospital. They had supported Nishith, who was running around the hospital all alone. Deepa was surprised Nalini had opted not to come on the discharge day either! Nishith said, "Amma has kept Appa's room ready, and she said she will receive him at home."

Deepa started visiting Nalini regularly. Sometimes Pranati drove her. On one such trip, Deepa was looking at Nalini's drawn face. She could not help but ask, "Is everything fine, Nalini?" Just that one question was enough to break Nalini's dammed emotions. She started crying. Sobs did not stop for quite some time. Deepa let her cry to her heart's content. Pranati had no clue how to handle such outbursts. She stood there, dazed, looking at Deepa. Deepa seemed to know what to do and what to say—not say—in any situation. She felt awkward and walked towards Vikram's room.

As the sobs subsided, Deepa asked Nalini, "What would help you overcome your sorrow?" Nalini's immediate response was, "A bit of Vikram's attention," revealing a distance between them unnoticed by the family. Deepa, holding Nalini's hands, encouraged her to speak. Nalini began to share the complexities of her 25-year marriage, contrasting Vikram's public persona of kindness and spirituality with his indifference and lack of empathy at home. Over time, Vikram's growing focus on his business and external validation led to an emotional disconnect, leaving Nalini feeling neglected and unloved. Despite her efforts to communicate and seek a deeper connection, Vikram remained oblivious, causing Nalini to retreat into herself and find solace in her children. Deepa listened with empathy as Nalini described the gradual erosion of their relationship, from a once warm and connected marriage to a hollow routine filled with emotional void. Nalini confessed that the children, now grown, saw them as a harmonious couple, unaware of the coldness between their parents.

Deepa hesitantly asked Nalini, "Nalini Don't get me wrong. I am strongly sensing something else apart from all these issues between Vikram and you. You have been married for several years, and I am sure that these situations of becoming cold towards the other partner are like changing seasons. It will be set right. You are telling me all the symptoms in detail. You are not telling me the cause." This was a checkmate for Nalini. The one thing that she wanted to bury deep inside her heart and she didn't want to face it, Deepa had spotted and excavated!

It was a quiet evening, and with the sun casting golden hues through the living room windows, Nalini sat on the couch, her hands trembling slightly.

Deepa, noticing her change in expression, sat beside her, concern evident on her face. Deepa gently asked if everything was alright and placed a comforting hand on Nalini's shoulder. Nalini took a deep breath, trying to steady her voice. She had been holding onto this secret for too long, and the weight of it was crushing her spirit. She knew she had to confide in someone, and Deepa, with her kind and understanding nature, was the right person. Nalini began to speak, her voice quivering. She told Deepa that there was something she needed to share, something about Vikram. Deepa's eyes widened with worry, and she asked if Vikram was alright. Nalini shook her head, tears welling in her eyes, and explained that Vikram was fine, but it was about their marriage. She had found out that Vikram had been having an affair.

Deepa gasped, her hand flying to her mouth in shock, and asked With whom. Deepa had suspected this and had probed Nalini after seeing their weak chemistry. Nalini mentioned her name, Nisha, and added that she worked in Vikram's office. They had similar interests that had brought them very close. Deepa's face softened with empathy, and she asked her how she found out. Nalini looked away, recalling the heart-wrenching moment when she had been cleaning the house and decided to tidy up Vikram's cupboard. She found a gift wrapped beautifully and a letter tucked inside. When she read the letter, she realized it was from Nisha. She wrote about how much she enjoyed spending time with him and felt a deep connection with him. Deepa listened intently, her heart breaking for Nalini, and commented, "It must have been hard to read." Nalini admitted, "Yes, it was. I felt like the ground had been pulled out from under my feet. Since then, I have noticed how Vikram has been drifting away from me, showing less interest in conversations and spending more time at work or out with 'friends. Just not that, I used to see the spark in his eyes when he talked about Nisha—that look he used to have for me was shifting towards Nisha. It was unbearable."

Deepa squeezed Nalini's hand and asked, "Have you spoken to Vikram about it?" Nalini said, "I tried, but he denied everything, accusing me of imagining things and being paranoid. However, I know what I saw and felt—the growing distance between us, like he is slipping away and there is nothing I can do to stop it." Deepa hugged Nalini tightly and said, "Nalini, I am sorry for what you are going through, but dear, you didn't deserve to feel this way. What have you planned to do now?" Nalini whispered, "I don't know Deepa. I have to admit that this has made me start losing belief in marriage. I used to think we were happy and our love was strong enough to overcome anything, but now I feel like everything I believed in was a lie. I don't know how to move forward." Nalini recalled, "According to a staff member, Vikram had a huge fight with Nisha that evening. It must have taken a huge psychological toll on him. Later that night, he had a cardiac arrest." Deepa held Nalini, offering her silent support, and assured her that whatever she decided, Deepa would be there for her and they would get through this together. Nalini felt a glimmer of hope, knowing she wasn't alone. With Deepa by her side, she could begin to navigate the difficult road.

No one had told Vikram that his wife did not come immediately to the hospital. He was still deluded about his place in his family. As the distractions started waning and he was confined to his room for months of recovery, he started seeing the distance between him and Nalini. The conversations were abrupt. She seemed to be busy with her circle of friends and family. He was not going out, and very few people from the business circle had time to come over and meet him. Time was money in his world. He started craving warm human company. He had not built a good circle of close friends, as he mistrusted everyone. The freeloaders, whom he had thought would come running, were busy building other resources. He was, after all, one of the many resources. His children were loving but had their own world.

The illness was eroding layers of his delusion. He had not built anything of value for himself or his family. Wealth, yes, but that can be earned. What was his contribution to his family? Would they even miss him if he died? He wanted answers. He was tired of his image and tired of living for others. He realized he no longer knew himself.

Despite Nalini having grown hard-hearted towards her husband Vikram due to past grievances, she continued to care for him without any expectations.

Every day, she attended to his needs with gentle devotion, her actions speaking louder than any words of reproach ever could. Vikram was observing her unwavering kindness and was filled with remorse for his actions.

Nalini noticed the changes in Vikram and was observing, curious, and compassionate. Vikram had not called anyone in days. He started relishing his food again. He had developed the habit of eating what was served without saying a word. He even complimented her cooking regularly—not done in decades of marriage. She saw the coldness in her heart reduce, and hope rekindled in her that they may still have a chance as a couple. Maybe they can sort out the differences this time around without pretense.

One evening, overwhelmed by Nalini's kindness, Vikram approached her with tear-filled eyes, and without saying a word, he embraced her tightly, like a child seeking comfort. With that heartfelt hug, he poured out his feelings, expressing deep regret and vowing never to take her for granted again. "You are precious to me, Nalini," he whispered, "and I will never lose you again."

After venting out, Nalini became light, but Deepa was feeling very heavy after speaking with Nalini. She thought to herself, "After 25 years of marriage, a woman who has always believed her husband to be her world will feel utterly devastated upon discovering his affair. This revelation shatters her trust and the foundation of her life, leading to a profound sense of betrayal and heartbreak. The emotional security and the deep bond she thought they shared are suddenly called into question, making her feel unloved, undervalued, and deceived. I am sure her self-worth takes a hit as she grapples with feelings of inadequacy and questions her perception of their relationship. The pain of infidelity is always compounded by the years of shared memories and commitment, leaving her to navigate a tumultuous sea of anger, sadness, and confusion as she reassesses her marriage and her future."

Deepa had not said anything to anyone at home—surprisingly, not even to Girish, with whom she would not hide anything. Though she saw that her respect for Vikram had gone down, she decided not to rush to any conclusions. She prayed sincerely for Nalini and Vikram. She was sure Girish was sharp enough to catch Nalini's sadness. She felt Girish would not be able to forgive Vikram if he came to know about the matter.

Deepa had invited Nalini and Vikram for an evening family chit-chat. She was making evening snacks on a rainy day. Girish silently came beside her to help her and said, "Very thoughtful of you to help Nalini sort out whatever she was going through. I know she was relying heavily on Vikram to be happy. Her moods varied based on his behavior. His heart attack must have left her without any emotional support to rely on." Deepa had a question on her face about whether Girish knew everything. Girish said, "Yesterday, Nalini took me to a temple, and she told me everything. I am proud of you, Deepa, for the way you have helped her and, at the same time, managed the sanity and dignity of the family. Let Amma not know about this. She can't handle it at her age. Certain things look good as secrets, so let them vanish as secrets. It will be hard for me to forgive Vikram. But I'm seeing an opportunity to practice what I learned from the scriptures, not to carry grievances. Anyways, the dark phase is over for Nalini!" While saying this, Girish pulled Deepa gently towards him and patted her back to express appreciation and gratitude. Deepa smiled and said she had done what a true friend would do—that too, Nalini was family.

Girish said, "The belief that marriage is a universal problem solver is a misguided notion held by many, both women and men. It is the responsibility of each individual to manage their emotional well-being rather than relying on their spouse to provide happiness and fulfillment all the time." Girish pointed out that holding one's partner accountable for personal emotional states is unfair and unrealistic. Instead, there must be introspection, encouraging each partner to reflect on their own needs, desires, and mental health. By taking ownership of their emotions, individuals can foster a healthier and more balanced relationship, free from misplaced blame and unrealistic expectations." Deepa was amazed by Girish's statement. Girish continued, "We are with a certain set of people because of karmic debts (Runa in Sanskrit). The connections and mutual understanding we experience with others are influenced by our past actions and the spiritual lessons we need to learn in this lifetime. I strongly believe that when two people truly comprehend each other's emotions and perspectives, it is not merely a coincidence but a karmic bond that brings them together for growth and enlightenment. This perspective implies that the empathy and understanding we share with others are part of our spiritual journey, destined by our karma, guiding us towards deeper connections and self-awareness." Deepa was completely immersed in what Girish was saying. She lightened the air by pulling his leg. "I can already see Prakasham, Version 2." They both laughed. Girish said, "I am not even in that frame yet. I am taking baby steps towards understanding the scriptures. These instances are opportunities to practice what I learn."

They could hear a car stopping in front of their house, and Deepa came out. She was relieved to see a gentle smile on Nalini's and Vikram's faces. She felt that they had rekindled that friendship in their marriage, which is like an adhesive for any relationship to last. The family gathered near the dining hall for tasty snacks and hot tea, covered in a blanket of love and comfort. Deepa observed that there were no dramatic declarations typical of Vikram. He was genuinely participating in the conversation, listening intently. Girish also noticed the change. Girish was taken aback when Vikram mentioned he wanted to learn more about the Vedic way of living, respecting all creatures, and a balanced life of justice and harmony. He was genuinely happy to see the transformation. They had their differences, and Girish had never agreed on Vikram's way of doing business. Not all means justify the end, he would argue. As he talked to the new Vikram, he saw that he was keen on learning. He was no longer jumping to his point. He was not vehemently defending anything. As a curious student of life, Girish concluded that hospitals have a way of smashing egos.

8. The Perfect Disaster

Pranati had applied for a new job in India. A technical issue in the company caused Pranati's reporting time to be delayed by two months. She was happy as she got time to participate in her brother Pranav's wedding without the stress of the vacation ending and rushing back. Pranav's was a love marriage. He had liked Chitra while they were studying for a master's degree together at the university. His marriage was marked by tension and discord, contrasting starkly with the harmonious marriage of Pranati. The event was marred by the contrasting nature of the two families: Pranav's family was pompous and fun-loving, and his fiancée Chitra's family was a group of rigid perfectionists who scrutinized every ritual and pointed out mistakes. This created a silent undercurrent of dissatisfaction, particularly for Sudha, who felt the mismatched vibes. In this context, she fondly recalled Pranati's wedding, which was smooth and joyful, largely due to the efforts of Deepa and Girish, who adeptly managed and harmonized the proceedings.

Two months rolled by, and Pranati reported to her new job. She was happy and comfortable, as her office was close to her house. This reduced her travel stress in traffic jams in a busy city like Bengaluru. Before going to the office, after winding up with her morning routines, she would have a lot of time, and she would get quality time with Girish. Pranati loved to talk to Girish, as there was always something to learn from his profound thoughts and experiences. Over time, her father-in-law had become a friend, philosopher, and guide to Pranati. On a Friday morning, Girish and Pranati were grafting plants. Girish asked Pranati, "Pranati, is everything well at your mother's place? Did the new bride settle down?" Pranati herself was not clear on the answer. She answered vaguely. "Yes, hmm.. must be. I think so." Girish smiled at Pranati and said, "Why are you so unsure? They had a love marriage, right?" Pranati gave a weird smile and kept quiet.

Pranati, despite being comfortable in her husband's home, felt a deep unease as she observed her mother's struggles to adjust to the new dynamics brought on by her brother's marriage. Her mother found it challenging to accept her son's shift in priorities as he devoted more time to his new wife. The presence of the new daughter-in-law introduced a change in the household's balance, which Pranati's mother had difficulty reconciling with. This tension between the old and new relationships created palpable discomfort for Pranati, who was caught in the middle, empathizing with her mother's feelings while understanding the natural progression of her brother's married life. Pranati wanted to share her turmoil with someone.

It was a Saturday, and the sun shone brightly on the beautiful lilies in Girish's garden. He was admiring them and was trying to capture the floral beauties by zooming them through a DSLR camera lens. The lens captured Pranati sitting in the corner of the garden chair like a gray cloud. Girish walked towards Pranati and asked, "Pranati, what happened? Such a beautiful day, and you look gloomy." Pranati said, "Nothing, Appa." Girish said, "See, you are not good at lying, and I am too good at catching a lie. Come on, tell me what happened." Pranati expressed the disharmony that had started at her mother's place. Just then, his close friend, Dr. Sridhar, a renowned psychologist, walked in to meet Girish. Girish warmly greeted him and introduced Sridhar to Pranati, saying, "Pranati, this is Dr. Sridhar, my childhood pal." With a friendly gesture, Sridhar smiled and wished Pranati. Girish said, "Sridhar, so good to see you back from Europe. How are your son, daughter-in-law, and grandson doing? I hope you had a comfortable stay. We missed you at Shreyas's wedding." Girish remarked, "Pranati, he is one amazing person who has answers for everyone's psychological problems. All my friends call him the messenger out of the Bhagavad Gita." Pranati warmly invited Dr. Sridhar inside. Deepa was happy to see Dr.Sridhar. While serving coffee, through their conversations, Pranati learned from Dr. Sridhar that his clinic was just a kilometer away. She got the idea of asking her questions and discussing her discomfort regarding her mother with Dr. Sridhar.

That day, after Dr. Sridhar left, Pranati asked Girish, "Appa, can I talk to Dr Sridhar about my mother, Pranav, and Chitra? After the wedding, they are not at ease with their new life at my mother's house." Girish said, "Why not?" Girish sensed Pranati's unease and gently suggested, "Pranati, sometimes it's better to open your mind to an unknown person, like a psychologist. You do not have any personal connections or biases; you can speak freely without any hindrance. This often leads to solutions and insights you might never have considered. Dr. Sridhar has helped many people discover answers they never thought of by providing a fresh perspective." This advice resonated with Pranati, highlighting the value of seeking professional help to navigate her emotional and psychological challenges.

The next day, Pranati went to Dr. Sridhar's clinic. She waited in the lounge for half an hour. As Pranati sat in the lounge of Dr. Sridhar's clinic, she couldn't help but notice the impressive array of posters and quotes on human psychology adorning the walls. Each piece was designed with earthen aesthetics, exuding a sense of simplicity and grounded wisdom. The earthy tones and natural materials used in the decor created a calming and welcoming atmosphere. The thoughtful selection of quotes and their elegant presentation inspired Pranati, leading her to think Dr. Sridhar must possess deep insight and understanding. This reinforced her belief that seeking his guidance could truly help her navigate her emotional struggles.

The patient consulting Dr. Sridhar left, and Dr. Sridhar saw Pranati waiting in the lounge. Dr. Sridhar welcomed Pranati with warm hospitality. As soon as she entered, Pranati's eyes were drawn to a striking picture of the Gitopadesha, where Lord Krishna is mentoring Arjuna on the battlefield. Noticing her observation, Dr. Sridhar smiled and commented, "Meet the ultimate psychologist ever known to mankind. He provided the user manual for living a righteous life to the common man 5,000 years ago. People like us are psychologists for namesake." Pranati was amazed by Dr. Sridhar's humility and deeply impressed by his reverence for ancient wisdom. He offered her a seat and asked kindly, "So, Pranati, tell me, how can I help you?"

Pranati opened up; as she began to speak up, he interrupted gently with a smile, "Pranati, call me uncle. I'm more like Girish's family. 'Doctor' sounds too formal." Pranati smiled back and continued, "Uncle, my brother Pranav married recently. He stays with my parents. Pranav married Chithra, a girl he met while they were working together. Their company sponsored their higher education abroad, and during those two years, they grew very close. He always told me that Chithra would be a perfect fit for our family, not just for him.

Earlier, Pranav was humorous, full of life, and capable of cracking jokes with every statement. Chithra, on the other hand, is serious and a perfectionist. I think she was brought up with rigid dos and don'ts. She believes in stern discipline, keeping everything in its place all the time. It was evident during the wedding!

My mom, on the other hand, does not insist on protocols. She's happy if her kids are happy and aren't very demanding. She believes her children are as independent as her. She doesn't understand that some of us, even as adults, need emotional support. Pranav sees Chithra as a firm anchor for the family.

These days, both Pranav and Chithra have started working again. Since they returned to work, I've noticed Pranav facing normal family conflicts. My mom, the easy-going mother-in-law, and Chitra, the rigid perfectionist daughter-in-law, represent two contrasting ways of living. My mom values a relaxed and flexible approach, enjoying spontaneity, while Chitra insists on strict schedules, meticulous attention to detail, and perfection in every task. This difference has led to a silent suffocation as they struggle to adjust to each other's ways. My mother feels stifled by Chithra's relentless need for precision, while Chithra becomes increasingly frustrated by what she sees as my mom's lack of discipline and structure. This isn't healthy for their relationship. Over time, this silent conflict will erode their harmony, creating tension in their daily interactions. Pranav struggles to manage two irritated women. He tries to explain Chithra's standpoint to my mom. But Amma has concluded that Chithra is rude and disrespectful towards her. Chithra refuses to change her ways and says, 'Why should I change how I speak? I cannot keep changing to keep everyone I meet comfortable.' Pranav wants some peace at home after coming back from work." Pranati sighed, looking at Dr. Sridhar. "Uncle, I don't know where this is heading."

Pranati continued, "I have also observed that Pranav now parrots whatever Chithra says. He is slowly molding himself into whatever Chithra wants him to be. Any relative inviting them gets the standard answer, 'I'll check with Chithra and let you know.' In his view, Chithra is always right. He speaks of her as someone who works hard and has the family's best interests at heart. He paints her rudeness as frankness. I have tried my best to build a rapport with Chithra. When I call her, she complains about my mom and her way of doing things. I can see that Chithra is task-oriented. Sometimes, I feel she is afraid to show her human side.

You know, these days, my parents' first circle of relatives have started talking about Chithra. They are not comfortable coming home, as they feel that they are judged by Chitra strongly through her snarky comments. Pranav would try for a regular, free flow of conversation, but he senses the vibes from Chithra that will be putting people off. He wants her to know her new family and become one of them. The more he tries, the more people feel sorry for him. He is unable to understand that people rarely change. People are seeing the writing on the wall. Pranav is not himself anymore, appearing like a mere shadow of Chithra."

Dr. Sridhar interrupted gently, "Pranati, your attachment to them makes you feel down. Trust me, it's an equation between your mom and Chithra, and you are not part of it. Do not intrude; it will only worsen their relationship." Pranati nodded. "True, uncle, what you say is right. My parents are contemplating moving out of their own home, leaving it to their son, renting an apartment, and leading a peaceful life. Daily fault-finding is taking its toll." Dr. Sridhar could see Pranati's eyes filling with tears.

Dr. Sridhar asked, "Who do you think is causing the disharmony at home?". Pranati responded, "It looks like Chithra. She is younger and can adjust a bit. It is harder for elders to change at their age." Dr. Sridhar smiled, anticipating this response, as Chithra, being a new entrant and not a blood relative, would naturally be seen as the source of conflict. He continued, "Chithra was raised in a different environment. Naturally, she will need time to adjust to her new home." Pranati, reflecting, said, "Maybe my mother can be a bit more accommodating and let Chithra do what she wants." Dr. Sridhar smiled again. "Why should she? She is used to her way of doing things. This has been her home for years. She raised her children her way, and they have turned out fine."

Pranati, feeling more confused, pondered further: "Is it then my father? He is not interfering as the eldest and trying to find any compromise." Dr. Sridhar thought she was getting closer to the heart of the issue, but knew that identifying a single cause wouldn't solve everything. He explained to Pranati that with Sudhir, both Chithra and Sudha might not show the differences, but the underlying tensions would persist and grow over time when he doesn't take the lead and sort this issue as head of the family.

Dr. Sridhar then asked, "Who is most impacted?" Pranati immediately replied, "Pranav. Poor thing. He has stopped being himself. My heart goes out to him. He has to agree with whatever his wife says, answer our relatives, and defend her actions to my mother and my mother's words to Chithra. Yes, he is the one most impacted and suffering." Sridhar said, "Wait until he talks to you. They are newly married and will need time to adjust to each other and the families." Pranati decided to take his advice and observe for now.

Dr. Sridhar then explained, "Every strong human behavior has its roots in childhood and upbringing. The foundational experiences and environments a person was exposed to during their formative years significantly shaped their character, reactions, and behavior patterns. Before passing judgment or drawing conclusions about someone's actions, it's important to understand their background and the influences that have molded them.

This perspective encourages empathy and a deeper comprehension of individual differences, recognizing that behaviors often stem from past experiences rather than inherent flaws. By considering how someone was raised, we can appreciate the complexity of human behavior and approach others with greater compassion and insight." This explanation provided Pranati with a new perspective, and she decided to see the situation with more empathy and understanding. Pranati thanked Dr. Sridhar and told him she would need his help to handle this tussle. Dr. Sridhar smiled and said, "Psychologists enjoy tackling challenging problems, and you are always welcome to come to me for help." Pranati felt understood, valued, and less hesitant to seek his guidance whenever she needed it.

Chithra was getting more and more paranoid in her new role. The suffocation with Sudha was increasing day by day.

One Saturday evening, Pranati dropped into her mom's place. Sudha had gone to a friend's house. Pranati started conversing with Chitra; it was easier to speak with her alone than when Sudha was present. She began by bringing up common childhood scenes with Pranav, recalling nostalgic moments. Chitra connected with this and responded, "Really, childhood is fun. But I was not let loose in childhood like you people." This statement irked Pranati, but she paused and let Chitra continue. After the enlightening tips from Sridhar, she wanted to listen without jumping to conclusions.

Chitra rarely opened up about her feelings to others, but for a change, she started sharing. "As you know, my mother is a strict disciplinarian. When we were growing up, she wouldn't approve of anything we did. Her logic was that children wouldn't reach their peak potential if complimented for doing small things. I married Pranav against her wishes, and even now, I see her grim disapproval of my choice whenever Pranav and my mom meet. I feel the stress of seeking her approval for our marriage. I want to prove Pranav is the perfect match for me." Chitra continued, "My mother was not like your mom. She subjected Neela and me to harsh treatment throughout our childhood, enforcing strict rules and burdensome chores. We had to wash our clothes and clean our tiffin carriers ourselves—tasks uncommon for children our age. I used to feel jealous of other kids playing while their moms took care of their chores. Constantly, she scolded us and insisted we eat whatever was served without complaint, enforcing a rigid discipline that left no room for our childhood whims or preferences. Despite this relentless harshness, I am convinced my mother's methods were justified. We both value perfection."

"Aha!" thought Pranati. She got the clue to Chitra's behavior. Dr. Sridhar's advice made so much sense: the root of everyone's behavior lies in childhood! Pranati realized that Chitra had consoled herself into believing that her mother's strictness was a form of care and that enduring these hardships was essential for their good. Chitra had internalized her mother's perfectionist standards as necessary and beneficial.

Chitra's cold behavior had its roots in being raised by a cold, perfectionist mother. Their mother's relentless pursuit of perfection left little room for the carefree joys of childhood, imposing a strict routine that stifled their natural expression. Her childhood had stringent restrictions on playing and talking, and she could not express her feelings, even as an adult.

As Chitra spoke, Pranati felt a deep pang of empathy and sorrow, recognizing that such a severe environment must have suffocated the sisters' innocent delight and spontaneity, effectively killing the essence of their childhood. Pranati did not speak much and took her leave. Before leaving, Pranati said, "Chitra, can I say something? Of late, I can see that you, Amma, and Pranav are struggling to wade through at home comfortably. I think you can meet a psychologist. It will surely help. I am suggesting this so you might find solutions based on new perspectives. You can't discuss everything with family. There will be biases, and we will not be comfortable with their opinions." She handed over Dr. Sridhar's card. Chitra also felt that what Pranati said made sense. She already imagined, in her mind, Pranav and Sudha getting counseled!

The next day, she spoke to Pranav and suggested they meet a psychologist. If it were a premarital version of Pranav, his answer would have been a strict no. But now he was deluded, thinking that saying no to his wife was a sin! Chitra took Pranav to Dr. Sridhar. Dr. Sridhar asked, "Yes, madam, what brings you here?". Chitra started, "Pranati gave your reference, sir. I am her sister-in-law." Sridhar was seeing the character of his ongoing case study live! He said, "Sure, ma'am. Tell me, what is the matter? How can I help you?" Chitra started telling all the problems about her husband and in-laws! For Dr. Sridhar, it sounded as if he were a teacher listening to a parent's grievances in a parent-teacher meeting! Chitra, who was an innocent victim of childhood trauma and OCD related to cleanliness and strict protocols, started complaining to Dr. Sridhar about her Pranav and Sudha. She accused them of being irresponsible and careless in maintaining the home and their routines. Her frustration and anger were evident as she vented about their perceived shortcomings. Pranav, embarrassed and uncomfortable, tried to intervene and calm Chitra down, attempting to divert the conversation, but he failed miserably. Dr. Sridhar listened patiently to Chitra's complaints without interruption. Once she finished, he said, "Chitra, I now understand your problem. Can I now talk to your husband in private?" Chitra, feeling victorious for having aired her grievances, walked out of the cabin to the lounge. Inside, Pranav felt incredibly awkward and anxious facing the doctor. Dr. Sridhar reassured him, saying, "Pranav, you are fine. Your wife needs counseling. The problem lies there." Pranav was left speechless, as Chitra had made him feel he was entirely worthless.

Dr. Sridhar looked at Pranav and began, "Pranav, a person suppressed by a perfectionist parent, develops significant childhood trauma. This constant control and lack of freedom create deep-seated issues, making it difficult for the person to manage their anger and emotions later in life."

Pranav listened intently as Dr. Sridhar continued, "Chitra's strict upbringing and the unrealistic demands placed on her during childhood have likely caused her current struggles with OCD and emotional regulation." "So, what can we do about it?" Pranav asked with a hint of desperation in his voice.

Dr. Sridhar smiled reassuringly. "Once Chitra becomes aware of the root cause of her restlessness and OCD and starts addressing it through counseling, she will gradually learn to manage her emotions better. Her obsessive behaviors will significantly decrease over time. This awareness and the healing process will help her lead a more balanced and harmonious life." Pranav nodded slowly, absorbing the information. "Thank you, Dr. Sridhar. I hope she finds the help she needs."

He asked Pranav to wait outside and call Chitra in. Dr. Sridhar started, "Chitra, I need to ask you some questions to address the issue. There is no doubt your husband needs to be counseled. But marriage is a partnership. So I might have to ask a few things from you and suggest a few things to you. If you are open to that, we can start our sessions." Chitra liked his approach and agreed to meet him for further sessions.

Subtly and compassionately, Sridhar began counseling Chitra, helping her navigate the effects of childhood trauma caused by her domineering mother. Without directly confronting her about the trauma, he gently guided her through conversations that encouraged self-reflection and awareness. Sridhar's approach was so graceful that Chitra was unaware she was being counseled. He led her to understand that the challenges she faced in her relationships and her tendency to project faults onto others were deeply rooted in her past experiences. By fostering a safe and supportive environment, Sridhar helped Chitra recognize the importance of introspection. He gently guided her to look inward and address her unresolved emotions to find healing and personal growth. This subtle guidance paved the way for Chitra to start her journey towards self-discovery and emotional well-being.

In one of the sessions, Dr. Sridhar casually asked Chitra, "Can you narrate any one episode that has made you feel that it is a mirror situation of childhood? Is there anything that has caused you pain? I want you to narrate it." Chitra thought for some time and recalled, "I went to my sister Neela's place once. I am fond of my super-cute nephew. My sister, Neela, is married to Sujay. They have an 8-year-old son, Nishchal. Both of us live a few roads away from our parents' house. Once, Neela and her family had returned from a vacation during the school holidays, and Neela was still down from travel. I had prepared some breakfast for them and had gone to give it to them. As I opened the gate to their home, I saw my nephew sitting outside with a long face. I heard Sujay's raised voice. I started walking towards my nephew. I had never heard Sujay raise his voice in the 10 years since he married my sister. I was wondering what caused such an outburst." As and when Chitra started narrating, she got engrossed in that past situation! And she started narrating it from scene to scene, like a movie!

"I wanted to go in, but my curiosity got the better of me. As I stepped aside from the porch and sat on the sidesteps, I heard Sujay say, "Neela, this is too much. Nishu is hardly 8 years old. You stopped him from playing with kids his age. What will some dirt do? Kids develop immunity when they play outside. Do you see that he is getting afraid of you? You do not have a single good word for whatever he does. What was wrong with the painting he did at the resort? He had found a new flower and was trying to get the right color. Instead of helping, you started with a huge critique of how the colors do not match, coming out from the sides. Poor thing; he did not touch the painting brush after that. Same with swimming. Why did you tell him he did not get the perfect butterfly stroke after just a month of training? How would you know he will not get it tomorrow?" I was shocked, and I felt my heart melt for Nishu, and I helplessly stroked his hair.

Sujay continued, "Do you think you are the standard setter for everything and everyone around? I like to eat dosas hot from the tawa. But Mrs. Perfect's family eats together, even if they do not like cold, soggy dosas." Sarcasm was dripping from Sujay's words. "And yes, Mrs. Perfect is never wrong. You booked the resort. But, hey, when the swimming pool was not up to your standards of cleanliness, it became my problem.

I should've checked the reviews before coming. Well, adults take responsibility for their decisions. They are also decent enough to say sorry and not blame shift to protect their deluded perfectionist self-image."

I was surprised that my sister was not interrupting. I felt like rushing in and defending Neela. But being married for some time has taught me not to get into husband-wife fights. It will only get worse. Sujay was saying, "Have you noticed none of our relatives come home as frequently? Of course, it is my fault. All you do is talk endlessly about how to maintain a perfect home. When we visit others, we are not interested in building warm bonds. I get tired of the faults you list in people and their homes. Have you ever thought you have made our home into a hellhole without Nishu giggling or inviting his friends home? Do you think he will be the same all his life? In a couple of years, he will not be doing what he is doing now. When he grows up, he will not want to come home. I'm done. I will not be a mute spectator as you chip away at my son's self-esteem with your daily critique and fear-based parenting in the name of discipline. I'll be me from now on. No more covering your flaws by taking blame for whatever is not perfect according to you."

I saw an angry, red-faced Sujay walk out of the house, and Neela sank onto the sofa. I saw Nishu's eyes brim with tears, and I was reminded of a small, frightened rabbit as I looked at his face. I realized that my nephew at that time looked like a mirror image of my childhood version! The deep pain of childhood surfaced in me. With tears in my eyes, I walked out quietly. As tears started rolling down my face, I was seeing my childhood. My mother treated me the same way as Neela was treating Nishu. My mother always disapproves of Neela's parenting skills if Nishu did anything normal for his age, like climbing the compound. She blames Neela for the wrong parenting! My father is tired of his dominating and unruly wife and has given up on rectifying her. He is on mute.

By the time she finished her narration to Dr. Seedhar, Chithra was sobbing uncontrollably. Her fearful and anxious childhood had made her afraid of failure, unable to face challenges boldly, and fearful of going after what she wanted. She did not know what her heart wanted or how she would go about doing it. Her marriage was a rebellion of sorts. But she was still the same child, seeking her mother's approval. Her mind was in turmoil as she came back home. Every time after a counselling session, Chitra used to feel healed!

One Saturday, after Chitra returned from Dr. Sridhar's clinic, she saw Pranav with shoes next to him and reading a newspaper. He looked relaxed. As she entered, she saw that he was rushing to pick up the shoes. Without a word, she walked to her room. Pranav and Sudha were both shell-shocked. Pranav was expecting a nice 10-minute lecture on how every family member contributed to a clean home. Keeping the right-sized shoes in the right place in the shoe rack helped in the long run, on and on. He continued to read the paper, thinking she had not noticed the shoes.

Pranav was not keen on meeting Chitra's mother. The smirk of disapproval was not inviting. He would still go, as Chithra wanted to show they are a perfect couple who will not go anywhere without each other. He was hoping she would come out of her delusions and reach planet Earth soon. But as days passed, his hopes were waning. He was getting a bit tired of her hypocrisy. Many times, he felt like telling her not to compare her mother and mother-in-law, as they are different people and like chalk and cheese.

Chithra refused dinner and locked herself inside her room. No one knew what had happened. The next morning, as she came out, her eyes were swollen but clear. The bitter tears had washed away some of the built-in angst and trauma from childhood. She smiled at Sudha in the kitchen. Sudha was making idlis, and the batter had dropped on the countertop. She was busy making chutney without wiping the batter. Chithra took a cloth and wiped the batter. Sudha looked back. She wondered what had happened. Chithra was not preaching and was not getting irritated; Sudha thought it must be an auspicious day.

Chithra decided to be quiet and get to know her family. She was seeing her past with a new lens. She had decided to let go of many beliefs that were not serving her anymore. Why seek something she would never get? Her mother's approval. Her mother was getting grumpier with age. After counseling with Dr. Sridhar, Chitra realized that she was now in her home with a husband who was open to new ideas and suggestions;

her mother-in-law, though cautious about people, would prepare what they wanted with love; and it was easy to communicate with warm Pranati. Her smile became broader as she saw Shreyas and Pranati entering home. They had dropped by on their way back home after a walk.

She welcomed them and inquired about Sumathi and Deepa. Shreyas had heard she was prudish, judgmental, and not open to anyone from Sudha. Here, he was seeing a very different Chithra.

Chithra offered them coffee and snacks, and parceled a snack package home. The package was not just snacks; both Sudha and Pranav saw the warmth of Chithra's heart go with the parcel. Pranav hoped to see a friend in Chitra again!

9. Lost and Found

"Sometimes, the greatest love is found in the moment you realize what you've lost."

– Unknown

Pranati and Shreyas had gone out shopping. Shreyas saw his colleague Pradeep browsing in a bookstore. He walked up to him. "Hi Pradeep, how come you are here? Very far from home. Welcome to our area." Pradeep smiled. Chit-chat ensued, and Shreyas introduced Pranati to Pradeep. Pranati said, "Hello, where do you stay, Pradeep?" Pradeep said, "I am basically from Chennai. I have been working on many offshore assignments before moving here for a couple of years on a major project." Shreyas interrupted, "Pranati, He is an expert in his domain, and he loves traveling." Shreyas said, "Hey Pradeep, my home is just across the street. Please drop by for some coffee." Pradeep said "Thank you. But not today, Shreyas. I had to accompany Maya. So I came this way. I have some other work to do. I need to rush back. I will surely come over some other time." Saying that, he waved bye.

Pranati was curious. Pradeep looked to be in his mid-thirties or early forties. As far as men's conversations go, there was no hint of his family. The name Maya at the end of the conversation caught Pranati's attention. Seeing Pranati's curious eyes, Shreyas got ready for a questionnaire that would follow! Pranati asked, "Shreyas, I want to know about his family." Shreyas responded, "I was thinking why my madam Curie's curious questions are still not out!" Pranati gave a stern look at him. Shreyas smiled and continued, "Pradeep is an introvert. No one knows much about him in the office. A thorough professional respected for his skills and good manners. We have heard rumors that he is in a live-in relationship with one of our colleagues, Maya." Pranati's eyes sparkled as a CBI agent's success moment in solving a mystery! She said, "Oh, Maya, the one whom he went to pick up! Tell me more about Maya." Shreyas teased Pranati, "You are a gossip queen." Shreyas chuckled as he playfully teased Pranati, calling her a curious cat for always wanting to know the latest gossip. With a determined glint in her eyes, Pranati retorted like a stubborn child, "Yes, I have all the right to know whatever I want from you, Shreyas." Amused and affectionate, Shreyas smiled and said, "It's this inquisitive nature of yours, Pranati, that completely bowled me over!"

Shreyas continued, "Maya is academically accomplished and good-looking. A rare combination of beauty and brains. She was her college topper and earned the job based on her rank. She lives her life on her terms. She loves to party and has enough social contacts to be a regular fixture on *page three*. Do you know Pranati? She has a massive fan following on Instagram. She loves to share her life—what she did, where she went, and how she felt—daily with folks she has no clue about! I tell you, this is so absurd! People have taken the time to follow her; naturally, they would love to know everything about her. I heard from her close associates that her parents insisted on her wedding. She has fallen in love with her lifestyle, and she feels she is not answerable to anyone, has no responsibilities for others, and has no care in the world. Today is meant for her to enjoy her life to the fullest. She was very fit when she joined our office. Late-night parties, bad eating, and social drinking have not caused many problems. As she started pushing 30, she moved out of her parents' place as her lifestyle choices created constant clashes with their traditional way of living." Pranati didn't allow Shreyas to stop. "Now tell me about the Maya and Pradeep combo!" Shreyas smiled. "Your gossip quotient is high, Pranati!" Pranati insisted, "Shreyas, on this hot topic, you will stop if we reach the house. Come, let us take one more stroll till the end of the road, till you complete this topic." Shreyas said, "You are crazy!" Shreyas did not have any other option but to continue.

"Pradeep and Maya had gotten to know each other when working in our office on a stressful project. The hours were long. Pradeep would want to go home and rest. Maya would pull him away and go out for a drink. Over time, Pradeep started liking her unbridled personality. He is quiet and not very expressive. Opposites attract, and they are living together. As far as I know, Pradeep has not thought about marrying or settling down. He is passionate about work. His travel goals are his constant company. His family pressure is mounting, as he turned 37 last year. He is running out of excuses. He is not against marriage. But the convenient arrangement he has with Maya, I think, is working well. He likes her company and is not keen on planning anything at present. Maya is also not pushing him for marriage. Life is good at this point."

Pranati felt dumbstruck and shocked as Shreyas narrated the story of Pradeep and Maya's live-in relationship. Her eyes widened in disbelief, and her mouth fell open as she struggled to process the unexpected revelation. The idea of Pradeep and Maya, whom she had assumed as husband and wife in a different light a few moments ago at the bookstore, living together without marriage was completely jarring. Her mind raced, reconciling this new information with her previous perceptions, leaving her speechless and overwhelmed.

Pranati was not a supporter of noncommittal relationships, particularly open marriages. She harbored significant doubts about their dynamics, worrying that people could easily be taken advantage of in such arrangements. The lack of a promise for a shared future troubled her, as it meant that either partner could walk away at any time. She questioned whether all individuals were emotionally resilient enough to handle such breakups. Pranati also considered the scenario where one partner might develop genuine affection and long for a stable home, leading to inevitable heartbreak. Additionally, she pondered the implications of these relationships as people aged, contemplating the potential for loneliness and regret. Despite these heavy thoughts, Pranati set them aside to focus on her long to-do list before heading home.

Shreyas had not thought much about the consequences of live-in relationships. Pradeep and Maya were the first ones he knew of. He strongly opined that people can do what they want with their lives. It is their choice, and yes, they will be prepared to face the consequences of their choices. When they make a choice, they have thought it through and have their reasons. He was not someone who would clutter his head with irrelevant information.

On Friday, Pradeep met Shreyas in the office corridor. They exchanged smiles. Pradeep took a few steps forward, turned around, and said, "Shreyas, I will be coming to that bookstore again tomorrow. I will stop by your home if time permits." Shreyas said, "Very welcome, Pradeep. Have lunch with my family, and you can have some good local food." Pradeep said, "No formalities, Shreyas. I have some time between my lunch appointment and dinner. Will come in for a coffee around 4 'O' Clock." The next day, Pradeep called Shreyas and said, "Shreyas, we will come around lunchtime itself as my program got changed." Shreyas was puzzled when he said "we." Shreyas thought Pradeep was coming alone. Pradeep clarified, "Shreyas, Maya, and I are coming". Shreyas said, "Please do come, Pradeep. I look forward to seeing you both." When Shreyas told this to Pranati, she was flustered. "How can you simply ask them to come over? Ajji will ask them about their lives. You know she loves the company of new people and wants to hear the details. How will we manage? We'd better tell everyone." Shreyas said, "Don't worry so much. They may be used to such queries by now." Pranati was not convinced.

Thankfully, Sumathi left for her daughter Nalini's house in the morning. Pranati heaved a sigh of relief. She knew Girish and Deepa would not probe unless people shared their life histories voluntarily as part of a regular conversation. Pradeep and Maya came over for lunch. Maya was wearing a simple cotton sleeveless dress and simple makeup. They both looked very comfortable in each other's company. She gave a bouquet to Pranati. Girish and Pradeep got into a regular conversation about finance. Maya was bubbly and walked around the home, appreciating random pieces of furniture, Deepa's crockery set, and flowers in their garden, and wanting to know how Pranati manages her roles. Pranati was feeling a bit uncomfortable. She was not sure what topics to bring up and what to avoid. But Maya seemed to have no inhibitions. They were sipping coffee in the garden when she opened up about her life choices.

Pranati pretended to be innocent and asked Maya, "Maya, tell me more about yourself." Maya smiled and said, "I come from a traditional home. Until I graduated, I had not thought much about life. I wanted to land in a good job, use whatever I have learned academically, and be financially independent." Pranati complimented her, "You look so beautiful! Because of your looks, I am sure you would have had many admirers in college and the office." Maya was aware of the impact of her looks and enjoyed the attention, and with social media, she was getting more and more attention. Maya smiled at Pranati's compliment.

She continued, "Once I started working, I made friends with a girl called Charu. Charu thought that marriage was binding for a woman. She cannot grow as much in her career because of her children, and travel becomes limited. Her learning reduces over time. She will run a home, yes, but personal aspirations take a back seat. But Pranati, I had not thought much like Charu, but I always loved the idea of being free. But Charu's ideologies sound more logical, and I use this logic as an antidote whenever anyone asks me about my marriage."

Maya's eloquent style made Pranati doubt herself. Was she wrong about getting married? All her points sounded so logical and valid. Pranati asked feebly, "But what about the warmth of a home? Don't you want a safe place to come back to? What about raising the next generation? The ties of family?" Maya laughed and said, "I'm not the thinking type, Pranati. Life is fun at present. I have enough to spend on people who adore me, and I'm not answerable. What more do I want?". Pranati was getting even more confused. She wanted to draw a logical conclusion to their discussion. But just then, Pradeep pointed to the time, indicating it was getting late, and they both took leave.

At dinner time, Deepa asked, "Are Pradeep and Maya married?" Pranati blurted out, "How did you know they are not married?" Deepa was smiling. "You think we cannot make it out? A married couple is not so formal with each other. Pradeep asked her for her plans before confirming the evening appointment. She was not checking if he had his coffee and snacks. Also, Appa noticed that his financial planning did not have anything for his wife and kids. These are enough hints to guess". Pranati bowed dramatically and turned to Shreyas. "See, this is why I was saying we should tell everyone at home." She continued to tell their story and spoke about her confusion.

Deepa and Girish explained that a live-in relationship or an open marriage might not be the right choice because Pradeep and Maya aren't considering the long-term implications. Girish stressed, "Life is challenging and partners must support each other when things get tough. While Pradeep and Maya might feel certain now, the human mind can change unpredictably, making their decision risky. Pranati, I feel Maya needs some help to understand her parents' concerns and anxiety, especially as they age. Maya's actions are causing undue stress for her parents, who deserve peace in their later years. Pradeep seems capable of settling down if he chooses to. I feel he has the maturity for a stable relationship, but Maya needs someone who would encourage her to think more critically about her choices." Deepa added, "Here the primary concern should be to ensure long-term stability and emotional support between them. I strongly believe that only a committed relationship provides the best foundation for this." For Pranati and Shreyas, their advice seemed to aim at fostering deeper reflection and consideration of future consequences.

It was a Sunday morning, and Pradeep was admiring and watching Maya as she said she got a 150th like for her recent photo. He was curious and asked Maya, "Why does the number make you so happy?" Maya thought and did not have an answer. As Pradeep had pointed out multiple times, she did not know why the person "liked" her or why "no likes" on social media made her unhappy. How many times has she liked anyone's photo? She would say she had no time. And do several likes matter, or do they come from specific people? She would normally brush aside these questions. But today, after visiting Shreyas and Pranati, she was thinking. Pranati seemed to enjoy her home. She was also working. Was she missing something?

The positive vibes and warm family atmosphere in Shreyas and Pranati's home were soothing for Pradeep and Maya. Being immersed in a loving and supportive environment, Pradeep and Maya began to notice the stability and happiness that Shreyas and Pranati shared. This contrast to their relationship dynamics prompted them to reflect on what they might be missing.

As they spent more time in this nurturing environment, Pradeep and Maya started questioning whether their relationship had the depth and mutual support that characterized Shreyas and Pranati's marriage. They observed how small acts of kindness, shared responsibilities, and open communication strengthened the bond between Shreyas and Pranati, leading them to realize the importance of these elements in a fulfilling partnership.

Pradeep felt very welcome in their home. The conversation was free-flowing. No one was trying to impress anyone. They were their natural selves. Secure was the word that was ringing in his head. He was feeling a bit insecure of late. He genuinely liked Maya and was feeling more drawn to her. Though they had chores split properly, he would not mind extending some of hers when she would wake up late after heavy partying at night. She would smile sweetly and thank him. He had begun to enjoy that smile.

His family was insisting he get married. He was feeling a bit lonely when Maya went off on her adventures. He loved music, sports, books, random surfing, and reading subjects like alternative medicine; nothing was filling that void. He had moved out of his home for his studies, and then his career had become big. He was a good cook and had maintained an efficient house for years. He did not have many friends. He was traveling a lot, but he had no time for deep connections. Of late, he was missing the little things about home. His mother screamed about waking up late and eating before having a bath. His father gets his favorite type of mango when it is in season and insists some be set aside for him. His aunt took him to her place, and he enjoyed treks with his cousins. He knew all of them had their own worlds. He felt grateful that they had shared something precious with him. Digital fatigue was setting in. He wanted to be more natural and flow with life without too many ideas about living cluttering his head. He was himself surprised by his thought flow. Life has its twists and turns.

He was wondering if he was falling in love with Maya. Well, his head had decided on a non-committal arrangement. But being with her and looking after her small needs made him happy. He wanted to build something of value together. The heart does not listen to the head, he sighed. While all these thoughts were running through his mind, Maya came out dressed up in her sporting attire with a backpack. Pradeep immediately questioned, "Where are you going? Why suddenly?" Maya smiled and said, "Why are you acting like a husband, Pradeep? I am off on an adventure trip with my friends. I might get a parcel that I was awaiting from Amazon. Please collect it. Bye." Pradeep was a bit disturbed. "For how long are you going?" She said she would return after a week!

When Maya went off on her adventure trip, Pradeep found himself unexpectedly missing her presence deeply. Without her laughter, conversations, and the small routines they shared, he realized how integral she had become to his daily life. The house felt emptier and less vibrant without her, prompting him to reflect on the moments they had spent together and the emotional connection they had built. As he thought about her, he recognized how much he valued her companionship and how her adventurous spirit and caring nature had enriched his life. This period of separation made Pradeep acutely aware of his growing feelings for Maya and solidified his realization that he wanted more than just a casual relationship with her. But he was scared to express this to her.

Maya returned the following Sunday. Maya had thought about Pradeep a hundred times. She was wondering why! One week had sounded like a month to Pradeep. Maya found that Pradeep had packed his suitcases. She asked, "Now where are you going?". Pradeep smiled and said, "Now why are you acting like a wife, Maya? I am going on my onsite office work to London. I will be back after 15 days." Maya's face shrank, and Pradeep's eyes caught that! They both wanted to express that they missed each other. But it got stuck in their throats!

The cab arrived, and Pradeep left. During the 15 days Pradeep was away on his on-site trip to London, Maya was missing him intensely. In his absence, she recalled their moments together—the comforting routine of shared meals, the laughter over inside jokes, and the quiet companionship that had become a staple of her life. Each evening, she waited eagerly for his phone calls, her heart skipping a beat every time the phone rang, feeling like a perfect wife anticipating her husband's return. As the days passed, she realized how much Pradeep had taken on in their relationship, managing responsibilities and making her life effortlessly smooth. His thoughtful actions, like ensuring bills were paid on time and taking care of household tasks, made her feel stable and supported, which she now deeply appreciated. This period of separation helped Maya recognize Pradeep's importance in her life. She saw him not just as a partner but as someone who genuinely cared for her well-being, like a responsible husband.

Maya was a bit withdrawn when she attended a socialite event after meeting Pranati. She would blend in with the surroundings and would be the life of any party. She looked around, listening to conversations about money, status symbols, gossip about who and who, fashion, and charity events. She felt strange, listening to music and dancing with strangers. What was she doing here? Is this not what she has wanted all her life? Freedom to do whatever she wanted, whenever she wanted. Why is there a doubt that this is not sustainable, and she does not belong here? She remembered Pradeep, who would say that too much of anything is like burning down our home for warmth. Was she getting burned out? She was not extracting as much joy from the same activities. Earlier, one party a week would give her a dopamine high. After years, it was 3 to 4 per week. She had to keep upgrading her wardrobe to be relevant in these circles. Though she earned enough and more, she would feel guilty about spending. Her father's prudent warning would ring in her ears. She was not getting any younger. A pensive Maya left the party at 10. Pradeep opened the door and smiled. "It looks like you are becoming responsible. This is not you!" She smiled back. Sleep eluded her that night. A thousand thoughts of what she wanted raced through her mind.

Maya could not stay at home that day without Pradeep. Maya was no longer enjoying late-night parties as much. Most of her friends from college were married with children. One of her friends, Charvi, called her to spend a Sunday with her. Charvi was almost a family friend. She had heard Maya's mother complain about Maya's choices spoiling her health and life itself. Maya was happy to go to her place. Charvi had a 2-year-old son. Maya picked up a toy and some chocolates and went to meet Charvi. Charvi invited her inside and told her family had gone to their native. Maya was a little relieved; she felt she could have quality time with Charvi and be free and comfortable. As she saw Charvi run around to meet the demands of a naughty two-year-old, Maya was thinking, "Is this what I'm missing?" She saw Charvi grumble that she did not have much time with a child at home and that her home was a mess. But Maya saw her bright smile with a cautionary no when interacting with her son. She saw the love and warmth in her friend's home. A child does so much for a home. Maya enjoyed playing with the child.

She realized it was 5 in the evening when the next-door neighbor came over to invite Charvi to a festival. She extended the invite to Maya as well. Maya saw that the festival made her miss her parents. Her mother would celebrate every festival with devotion. She had enjoyed every one of them with relatives and friends. As they started to leave, her mother's friend, Revathi Aunty, walked in. She was happy to see Maya and started talking about finding a nice guy for her. She asked if she had found one herself. She smiled and said she would let her know first. She decided to meet her parents in the evening.

Maya dreaded meeting them these days. They were growing old and were worried about her. Her relatives were tired of finding a match for her. They had stopped advising her. Her mother was quiet, and her father looked serious. Her father openly said he never expected to raise a wayward daughter. Her mother started crying, saying that she had committed some serious sin. Maya had tried to keep her live-in relationship a secret from her parents. They had come to know and were upset. She understood that they were concerned. But she had fought many such battles before moving out. But this time, she felt guilty. She apologized to her parents and told them, "Very soon, she will be setting right her life so their agony will be relieved." This triggered a ray of hope for Maya's parents. She said goodbye to them and came back home.

That entire week, she was drowning in her thoughts. "Am I so selfish that only my pleasures matter?" As she entered her empty house, she remembered she had to pay the maid. Pradeep would take care of salaries, bills, and groceries. She would pay the amount. Sometimes, he would not tell her where he had spent the money. She remembered him with fondness. He had no reason to do the things he did for her. There was no binding. It was not a formal relationship. Simple things like packing her favorite chat because she would come home hungry. She was missing his kind presence. She could be herself around him without any pretense. He had accepted her with all her flaws and even seemed to enjoy many of them.

Saturday night, she stayed at home. Something she had not done in years. She would wonder how Pradeep spent so much time by himself at home. She had tried to pull him to her parties. He would say he preferred the company of familiar books to that of strangers. He had helped her sort out her finances, invest for the future, and remind her to save for a rainy day. Why was she missing the things that Pradeep said? The same things would make her bored when her father would caution. A good night's sleep made her wake up fresh in the morning. She went to the kitchen and made a fresh cup of coffee. It felt nice not to rush for an appointment, a party, or anything. A whole day with oneself. As she prepared breakfast, she thought Pradeep liked dosas with podi. She was seeing how he had become a major part of her life. She spent the afternoon thinking about her life as a whole. What would she do in her 40s? She was already getting bored with her lifestyle. In the 50s, did she not want to argue with a teenager? Normal things that people do seem so magical. She thought of proposing to Pradeep: "It is fine if he does not want to marry me. But I will ask him. I want to share my life with him. I want a warm home. That is what I'm missing."

As the day of Pradeep's return from London approached, Maya couldn't contain her excitement. She stood by the door, glancing out every few minutes, her heart racing with anticipation. She had prepared his favorite meal, wanting everything to be perfect for his homecoming. Meanwhile, Pradeep, sitting in the cab on his way back, felt a growing sense of resolve and excitement. As he watched the familiar streets pass by, he thought about how much he had missed Maya and how deeply his feelings for her had grown. He realized he didn't want to spend another day without knowing she was his forever. Determined and filled with love, Pradeep decided that as soon as he saw her, he would propose and ask Maya to be his life partner, envisioning a future together filled with the same warmth and support they had already begun to build.

The cab arrived, and Pradeep came near the door with his luggage. With a rush of emotion, Maya embraced him tightly. They both felt an overwhelming sense of belonging, as if they were always meant to find each other. The world around them faded away, leaving only the warmth of their love enveloping them. They realized that their connection runs deeper than they ever imagined. It's as though every moment they've shared has led them to this perfect instant, affirming that they are indeed made for each other. In that embrace, they find solace, joy, and the promise of a future filled with love and companionship.

Pranati and Shreyas were having lunch when the doorbell rang. They were pleasantly surprised to see Maya in a saree and Pradeep beaming. They entered with invitation cards in their hands. Pranati was very happy and hugged Maya. Deepa and Girish wished them well and hoped to see them settled in their cozy nest. Pranati was asking for the details of the proposal.

Deepa came to the kitchen to make coffee for them all. Girish came behind Deepa to help her. Deepa expressed her happiness over the decision taken by Maya and Pradeep. In his conversation with Deepa, Girish expressed, "Marriage is a profound institution — not a delicate arrangement easily swayed by passing impulses or fleeting desires. It draws its enduring strength from commitment, mutual respect, understanding, and responsibility. Over time, individuals come to appreciate the significance of these values and their broader obligations to the community. The innate human instinct to nurture, to foster growth, and to secure the well-being of future generations goes far beyond biological impulses; it reflects a fundamental truth of our nature. The sanctity and longevity of marriage are upheld by these enduring principles, which ultimately contribute to the greater good of society. Every species aspires for its lineage to flourish — why should humans be any different?"

10. Courage Conquers All

"Courage is resistance to fear, mastery of fear—not absence of fear."

– Mark Twain

Sumathi's biggest concern was for her eldest daughter Indrani. Indrani's husband Dayanand, was a challenging presence in the family. Known for his narcissistic tendencies, he had an uncanny talent for virtue signaling, often projecting an image of moral superiority that masked his true nature. Dayanand was extremely dominating, always insisting that his decisions were final, regardless of their obvious flaws. He was stubbornly committed to his choices, even when they led to negative outcomes, and refused to acknowledge his mistakes.

Dayanand showed little concern for his wife, Indrani, and daughter Sahana, viewing the family as merely a status symbol. He constantly made disparaging remarks to undermine others' confidence and elevate himself. His interactions were exhausting for family members, who struggled to manage his behavior. Despite his harsh nature, they remained considerate of familial duty. His dominance in conversations and lack of genuine care created a tense atmosphere. His inability to foster positive relationships left everyone tired and frustrated. They continued to tolerate him out of respect for family ties, hoping for a change. Sumathi, although unworried about her other children, always feared for Indrani due to Dayanand's narcissism.

Indrani was deeply worried about her daughter Sahana's marriage. True to his nature, Dayanand saw the marriage as another symbol of pride, caring more about social status and recognition than Sahana's happiness or future. His disregard for her feelings left Indrani anxious and unsettled. She feared that his dominating and narcissistic tendencies would overshadow the important decisions ahead. Dayanand was likely to focus on superficial factors—prestige, appearances, and the groom's family's status—rather than Sahana's compatibility and well-being. Indrani knew that Sahana's future could be at risk if he continued to make decisions based on his skewed priorities.

Indrani lay awake at night, worried that Sahana might end up unhappy or trapped in a marriage chosen for all the wrong reasons. She feared that Dayanand's lack of empathy would prevent him from considering Sahana's true desires and needs. Her stress only grew with his refusal to listen to anyone, making it nearly impossible to reason with him. Indrani felt increasingly isolated, as the rest of the family—exhausted by Dayanand's behavior—also felt powerless to confront him. She longed for Sahana's marriage to be more than a trophy for Dayanand and instead a genuine step toward a happy, fulfilling life. Despite the odds, Indrani remained determined to protect her daughter's interests, even if it meant standing up to Dayanand's overbearing influence.

Sahana, a sensitive and beautiful girl with a humble nature, was deeply loved by everyone who truly knew her. But growing up under her narcissistic father, Dayanand, had forced her into a shell of fear. His dominating presence and constant criticism dimmed her spirit, leaving her with insecurities and deep anxiety. Though gentle and kind, Sahana struggled to trust others or express her true self, always afraid of judgment or conflict. The shadow of her father's behavior still lingered, making it hard for her to recognize her own strength and embrace her inner confidence.

When Dayanand told Indrani that he planned to enroll Sahana in an expensive VIP matrimonial service, Indrani was terrified. She knew he was always drawn to appearances over substance, easily impressed by style, status, and glossy profiles. Indrani dreaded the thought of him prioritizing high-status matches while ignoring what mattered most for Sahana's happiness. The idea of Sahana being pushed into a superficial world where her real qualities could be overlooked deeply unsettled her. She feared Dayanand's obsession with prestige would overshadow the need to find a partner who would truly care for and understand their sensitive daughter.

Dayanand was eager to begin the groom-hunt. "Indrani, this week we are going on a pilgrimage to a few temples I've listed. After that, it will be an auspicious start to search for a groom for Sahana," he declared.

Indrani responded gently, "I feel that online proposals should be our last option. First, let's explore through people we know. A bride or groom is not a commodity. We must check the family's background carefully. Please don't rush."

But Dayanand reacted harshly. He scolded her, accusing her of being influenced by her mother and brother—people he dismissed as old-fashioned and unfit for the modern world. He even expressed his constant fear that their so-called "negative influence" might affect Sahana, especially since she spent time with her grandmother and maternal uncle's family. His hurtful words left Indrani feeling isolated and deeply anxious about her daughter's future.

Sahana, meanwhile, was terrified at the very idea of marriage. The oppressive atmosphere at home and her father's overbearing nature had filled her with fear and uncertainty. She felt especially sad for her mother, who endured most of Dayanand's domineering behavior.

Her only refuge was the warmth she found at her grandmother Sumathi's home and in her uncle Girish's family. Their house was a comforting escape from the tension she faced daily. Dayanand's temper, his shouting, and his abrupt exits were a regular scene at her own home, leaving her constantly on edge.

At Girish's house, however, Sahana felt safe and uplifted. Her spirits were at their brightest when she discussed music and literature with Sumathi and Deepa, finding joy and inspiration in their company. Outings with Shreyas and Pranati brought her immense happiness, offering moments of carefree laughter she longed for. Being an only child, Sahana cherished her bond with her cousin Shreyas, who felt more like a brother than a cousin.

These moments with Sumathi, Girish, and their children were the highlights of Sahana's life—filled with the love, understanding, and positivity she desperately needed but seldom found at home

After Dayanand left, Indrani told Sahana, "Your father has decided on a pilgrimage. It is my misfortune that I need to bear his company. At least you don't have to suffer. Tell him you cannot take off from the office and stay for a week at Girish's house. Sumathi Ajji will be happy, and your office is close to their house. I know your father will start yelling, but I will manage." Sahana felt happy about spending a week at her granny's house but sad for her mother, who had to endure her father's taunts.

Girish's house had a cozy studio apartment in the outhouse, which became a hub of creativity and gatherings. Downstairs, the space was used for musical get-togethers, where family and friends shared their love for music. Shreyas often used this area for guitar jamming sessions with his friends, filling the air with melodies and laughter.

The first floor of the outhouse was rented to Saagar, one of Shreyas' friends. Saagar was a bachelor and a passionate writer, working with a top publishing company. His name, meaning 'sea,' was a perfect reflection of his personality—deep, vast, and full of hidden treasures. Saagar was a creative soul, deeply thoughtful and introspective. His interests spanned philosophy and spirituality, subjects he explored with the same depth as his name suggested. A voracious reader, Saagar also expressed himself through blogging and poetry, sharing his profound thoughts and reflections with a wider audience. Saagar's presence added a unique dimension to the lively atmosphere of Girish's home. His intellectual pursuits and creative endeavors often became topics of engaging conversations during the musical gatherings. For Sahana, Saagar's thoughtful and serene behavior provided another layer of comfort and inspiration in her sanctuary at Girish's house. His deep and philosophical nature made him a fascinating figure, adding to the rich tapestry of positive influences that Sahana cherished in her second home.

Saagar often found himself silently admiring Sahana in subtle, endearing ways whenever she visited Girish's house. One such moment occurred during a musical get-together in the downstairs area of the outhouse. As Sahana lost herself in singing a soulful melody, Saagar stood in a quiet corner, his eyes following her every move. The way her face lit up with passion and her voice effortlessly filled the room captivated him. He couldn't help but smile softly, appreciating her talent and the genuine joy she exuded.

Another time, Saagar observed Sahana as she discussed literature with Sumathi and Deepa. He was seated on the staircase, pretending to be engrossed in a book, but his attention was entirely on Sahana. He admired the way her eyes sparkled when she spoke about her favorite novels and the animated gestures she used to emphasize her points. Saagar found her intellect and enthusiasm incredibly charming, and he enjoyed these stolen moments of silent admiration.

During one of the casual outings to a nearby eatery with Shreyas and Pranati, Saagar tagged along. He watched Sahana's playful interactions with Shreyas, her laughter ringing out as they shared jokes and teased each other. Saagar's gaze would often linger on her, noting how her face brightened with each smile and how effortlessly she brought warmth and light to those around her. He admired her from across the table, careful not to let his fondness show too openly.

On quieter evenings, when Sahana would retreat to a corner of the garden with a book, Saagar sometimes observed her from his first-floor window. He saw the peace that reading brought her, the way she would occasionally glance up at the sky, lost in thought. These moments of serenity and contemplation resonated deeply with Saagar, who valued the same in his own life. His admiration for Sahana grew with each passing day, nurtured by these small, silent observations that he held close to his heart.

Saagar often visited Shreyas' home, and during these visits, he sometimes overheard the discussions about the narcissistic tendencies of Dayanand. Through these conversations and observations, Saagar realized that life was not easy for Sahana. Although he silently formed his opinions about the difficult circumstances Sahana faced, Saagar never openly discussed his thoughts or indicated his particular interest in Sahana.

Once, during the Ganapathi festival at Shreyas' house, the atmosphere buzzed with joy and activity. Sahana was busy helping Deepa and Pranati by attending to guests and distributing sweets. Draped in a bright yellow saree, Sahana moved gracefully, her face glowing with a mix of festivity and responsibility. Saagar, who had arrived early to help with the preparations, found himself unable to take his eyes off her. As Sahana handed out sweets to the guests, her laughter ringing through the air, Saagar was captivated. He watched her delicate movements and the way her eyes sparkled with joy and warmth. Lost in his admiration, he didn't notice Sumathi observing him from a distance. Sumathi had been watching the young people closely, her experienced eyes missing nothing. She saw the way Saagar's gaze followed Sahana, filled with admiration and silent affection. A soft smile spread across her face as she noted the silent, tender moment. Sumathi thought to herself that Saagar and Sahana indeed made a lovely pair, complementing each other in a quiet, yet profound way. However, her smile faded slightly as she began to consider the formidable obstacle that was Dayanand's adamant nature. Sumathi knew that her son-in-law Dayanand's personality could pose significant challenges to any potential match for Sahana, especially one whom he hadn't personally chosen or approved. The thought weighed on her mind, yet, for the moment, she chose to keep her thoughts to herself, continuing to observe the festival's joyous happenings. She silently hoped that somehow, things would work out for the best and that Saagar's silent admiration for Sahana might one day blossom into something beautiful, overcoming all obstacles.

Early in the morning, as the first rays of sunlight filtered through the trees, Sumathi was busy picking parijatha flowers in the garden. The air was filled with their delicate fragrance, and the atmosphere was peaceful. As she moved around the garden, she noticed Saagar sitting in the outhouse, engrossed in a book.

Curious, she walked over to him and asked, "What are you reading, Saagar?". Saagar looked up from his book and smiled. "I'm reading a scene from the Mahabharata, the Uttarakumara episode. It's fascinating how Arjuna displays immense courage and drags Uttarakumara to face the enemies head-on. I find Arjuna's bravery incredibly inspiring." Sumathi gave him a playful, knowing look. "I never knew you admired courage so much in someone." Saagar, slightly taken aback by her tone, gave her a puzzled look and asked, "Why do you say that Ajji?" Sumati's eyes twinkled with mischief as she replied, "Well, if you are so impressed by courage, then why haven't you mustered the courage to propose to Sahana yet? What are you waiting for?" Saagar was stunned. He felt a mix of shock, surprise, and a sense of being caught off guard. He opened his mouth to speak but found himself at a loss for words. Sumathi's comment had struck a chord, and he realized she had seen right through him. Sumathi chuckled softly at his reaction, her eyes warm with understanding. "Don't worry, Saagar. Sometimes, the greatest battles we face are within ourselves. Just remember, true courage is about facing those battles." With that, she turned and continued picking flowers, leaving Saagar to ponder her words and the path he might take.

One Friday afternoon, Indrani hurriedly arrived at Girish's house, her anxiety apparent in her hurried steps. She asked for her mom, Sumathi, who was sitting on the balcony, peacefully reading her Bhagavad Gita. Indrani rushed up to her, her face clearly showing that something was deeply bothering her. Sumathi looked up from her book, immediately sensing the distress in her daughter Indrani's expression. "Indrani, what happened?" she asked with concern.

Indrani took a deep breath, trying to calm herself before speaking. "Amma, it's about Sahana. Dayanand has found a marriage proposal for her on an online VIP matrimony site. The man is supposedly the son of a former minister. Dayanand didn't consult me or Sahana about this, but he's already given his approval and moved things forward on his own. I'm really worried. I don't think this is right for Sahana at all." Sumathi's face darkened with irritation at the mention of Dayanand's unilateral decision. "This is unacceptable," she said firmly. "It's extremely risky to trust these online matrimonial sites without thorough scrutiny. There are so many cases of flawed proposals and deceitful profiles." Indrani nodded, her worry evident. "Exactly. I can't believe he didn't even think about consulting us. How can he be so reckless with Sahana's future?"

Sumathi placed her hand reassuringly on Indrani's arm. "In the past, parents would seek matches for their children in a much more careful and personal manner. They would rely on community connections, family references, and personal interactions to ensure the suitability of a match. It was a simple yet meticulous process, involving face-to-face meetings and thorough background checks. There was a sense of responsibility and care that ensured the proposals were genuine and well-suited." She paused, her eyes reflecting her deep frustration with Dayanand. "Dayanand's approach is hasty and irresponsible. Trusting an online profile without proper verification is a gamble with Sahana's happiness and future." Indrani sighed, feeling slightly relieved to have Sumathi's support. "What can we do, Amma? How do we stop this before it's too late?"

Sumathi thought for a moment before responding. "We need to talk to Dayanand together, present our concerns clearly, and insist that he halt this process immediately. We must emphasize the importance of involving Sahana in such a crucial decision and ensure that any future proposals are thoroughly vetted. Sahana deserves to have a say in her own life and happiness."

Indrani nodded, feeling more hopeful now that she had an ally in her mom, Sumathi. Sumathi, determined to stop Dayanand's reckless decision, went to Indrani's house with her son Girish and daughter-in-law Deepa. Their mission was clear: convince Dayanand not to proceed with the unknown marriage proposal for Sahana. However, when they confronted him, Dayanand reacted with hostility and humiliation, dismissing their concerns and sending them away. Sumathi and Girish maintained their composure despite Dayanand's negative reaction, but Deepa was visibly hurt by the confrontation. As they walked away from the house, Sumathi and Girish comforted Deepa. "It's what we expected from him," Girish said with a sigh, trying to soothe Deepa. They called Indrani aside and reassured her. "We'll figure out something to ensure this proposal doesn't proceed further." Sumathi promised.

On the drive back, a heavy silence filled the car. Sumathi, deep in thought, inadvertently let slip,

"The only way now is for Sahana and Saagar to elope. Otherwise, Dayanand will get Sahana married to that minister's son!" The revelation hit Deepa and Girish like a thunderbolt. Girish, in shock, abruptly applied the brakes, bringing the car to a sudden halt. Deepa and Girish both turned to Sumathi, exclaiming, "What!". Realizing what she had just said, Sumathi bit her lips, feeling a mix of regret and resolve. Girish, his voice filled with incredulity, asked, "Amma, what are you saying?"

Taking a deep breath, Sumathi explained her observations. "I've noticed how Saagar looks at my granddaughter Sahana, and it's clear he has deep feelings for her. They make a nice pair. I've seen the silent admiration in his eyes and the way Sahana seems at ease around him. It's obvious they care for each other." Deepa and Girish listened, absorbing this new perspective. Sumathi continued, "Dayanand's decision to marry Sahana off to someone she doesn't know or care for is reckless and unfair. Saagar and Sahana deserve a chance to find happiness together, without the interference of villain Dayanand." Girish, still processing the information, nodded slowly. "If Saagar truly cares for Sahana and if Sahana feels the same way, then maybe they do have a chance together. But eloping... It's a drastic step." Sumathi sighed. "I know, Girish. It's not an easy decision. But considering Dayanand's nature, it might be the only way to ensure Sahana's happiness. We need to talk to Saagar and Sahana, understand their feelings, and help them make an informed decision." Deepa, now calmer, added, "If this is the only way to protect Sahana from a life she's forced into, then we must support them. But we need to proceed with caution and ensure they understand the gravity of such a step." The car ride continued, now filled with a new sense of purpose. Sumathi, Girish, and Deepa knew they had a challenging road ahead, but they were united in their resolve to protect Sahana's future and happiness.

As Sumathi, Girish, and Deepa returned home, they gathered everyone to narrate the events at Indrani's house. Shreyas and Pranati listened intently as they heard about Dayanand's harsh reaction and Sumathi's unexpected revelation during the drive back. They were stunned, realizing that despite being around Saagar all the time, they had completely missed his feelings for Sahana. They were amazed at how well Saagar had hidden his love, even with everyone present. Pranati and Shreyas were elated at the prospect of Saagar and Sahana being together. Just then, Saagar entered the room to drop off the house keys before heading out. Pranati couldn't resist teasing him. "What, Mr. Romeo, how could you hide this from us!" Saagar blushed, feeling a mix of embarrassment and discomfort. Sumathi, sensing the opportunity, added, "It's time for you, Uttarakumara, to transform into Arjuna and take your bride away. Otherwise, you might miss the bus!"

Shreyas and Pranati stared at Sumathi in shock, impressed by her daring suggestion of eloping, especially since she was Sahana's grandmother, considering her age and traditional values. Saagar's face suddenly fell, showing his discomfort and unease with the conversation. Without saying a word, he quickly left the room, leaving everyone in stunned silence. Shreyas and Pranati turned to Sumathi, their expressions a mix of surprise and concern. "Ajji, are you really suggesting that Saagar and Sahana elope?" Shreyas asked, his voice filled with disbelief. Sumathi sighed, her resolve firm. "Sometimes, drastic situations call for drastic measures. Dayanand is forcing Sahana into a marriage she doesn't want, with someone she doesn't know. Saagar loves her, and I believe she cares for him, too. They deserve a chance at happiness, even if it means taking bold steps." Pranati nodded slowly, understanding the gravity of the situation. "But eloping is a big step. We need to talk to Sahana and Saagar, understand their feelings, and make sure they are prepared for the consequences." Girish added, "We must proceed with caution and support them in whatever decision they make. It's their future at stake, and they need to be fully aware of what they are doing." The family agreed, realizing that they needed to have a serious conversation with Saagar and Sahana. They would approach this situation with care, ensuring that both young hearts were fully prepared for whatever path they chose to take.

Saagar, disturbed by the news of the proposal for Sahana, called her and asked to meet on the premises of a nearby temple. When Sahana arrived and saw Saagar, she immediately started sobbing. Much to her surprise, Saagar raised his voice, saying, "This is not the time to cry, Sahana. It's time to stand up for yourself and clearly state your wishes to your father." The next day, Sahana informed Dayanand that she had invited Saagar to their home. Dayanand felt a sense of defeat, perceiving it as the biggest loss of his life. When Saagar arrived, Indrani received him warmly, but Dayanand refused to even smile; his discontent was evident.

Saagar, with his confident body language, looked like a brave lion to Dayanand. He walked straight to the point, requesting Sahana's hand in marriage. "Mr. Dayanand, I am well-planned in my life and ready for marriage. I have admired Sahana for her virtues and believe we can build a good future together." Dayanand scowled, murmuring to Indrani, "See, you used to trust your people and send your daughter to your sister Sumathi's house. Look at the result now!" Indrani, however, was unperturbed by his comments. Frustrated and feeling his ego bruised, Dayanand began to scold Saagar illogically. His tirade was fueled by his sense of defeat rather than any genuine concerns. Saagar listened patiently but remained firm. When Dayanand's rant finally paused, Saagar spoke calmly but with a steely edge, "Initially, I am requesting, sir. But please do not touch my sanity and wake up the beast in me. If you do not approve, my request will just turn into information."

Dayanand was dumbstruck by Saagar's confidence. He realized that Saagar was not intimidated by his outburst and was determined to stand his ground. The room fell silent, the tension thick in the air. Indrani looked at Saagar with a newfound respect, while Sahana felt a surge of pride for the man she loved. Seeing no way to shake Saagar's resolve and recognizing the determination in Sahana's eyes, Dayanand was forced to confront the reality of the situation. His attempts to control and intimidate were failing, and he was left speechless. Saagar, maintaining his composure, added, "I am committed to Sahana and our future together. I hope you can see past your pride and understand that my intentions are sincere and for the well-being of your daughter." With that, Saagar stepped back, waiting for Dayanand's response. Indrani, sensing the importance of the moment, gently placed a hand on Dayanand's arm, hoping to calm him and encourage him to see reason. Dayanand, still processing Saagar's bold stance, finally managed to speak, his voice lacking the usual arrogance. "I... I need some time to think." Saagar nodded respectfully. "Take all the time you need, sir. But know that my feelings for Sahana and my intentions remain unchanged." With the conversation concluded, Saagar took his leave, confident that he had made his position clear. As he walked out, Sahana felt a mix of relief and admiration for Saagar's unwavering support. Indrani watched Dayanand, hoping that this encounter would open his eyes to the strength and resolve of the young man who wanted to be a part of their family. He continued, speaking firmly but gently, "You must never play the victim. Today it's your dad, tomorrow it will be someone else trying to control your life. You have to pull back from this negative loop and clearly say what you want."

Sahana looked at him, stunned by his clarity. "I'm not that Bollywood hero who believes in eloping with his heroine. I want to inform your father and take you with his blessing, but for that, you need to be bold and ready to stand with me." He paused, then added, "Women should be the pillars of strength for the family, not weak chandeliers. Only when women are courageous can they steer the family in a positive direction. The energy of the woman is in the energy of her family." Looking deeply into her eyes, Saagar said, "I love you, Sahana. I've already accepted you as my life partner." His voice carried the authority, concern, and care of a husband, drawing Sahana even closer to him. Sahana heartily thanked Saagar deeply in her heart.

That evening, Sahana was lighting a lamp in the pooja room when Dayanand told her in a curt tone that the minister's family was coming home to see her. Sahana was unruffled, and she firmly told, "I don't want to proceed with the ex-minister's son's proposal. I am interested in Saagar, and I have already chosen him to be my future life partner." Indrani, standing nearby, was shocked by Sahana's courage, while Dayanand couldn't believe his ears. His face turned red with anger, and he switched to a narcissistic victim mode, attempting to emotionally blackmail Sahana into accepting the proposal. "How could you do this to me, Sahana? After everything I've done for you, this is how you repay me?" But Sahana stood firm, her voice unwavering. "Appa, I appreciate everything you've done, but this is my life, and I need to make my own decisions. Saagar is the one I want to spend my life with". Dayanand's anger flared again, but when he saw Sahana's determination, he realized he was losing control. He tried one last time, his voice laced with desperation, "You're making a big mistake, Sahana. You'll regret this." Sahana looked him in the eye and said calmly, "I won't, appa. I know what I want, and I won't let anyone dictate my life. Not now, not ever." Indrani, witnessing her daughter's newfound strength, felt a mix of pride and concern. Dayanand, seeing he couldn't sway Sahana, stormed out of the room, leaving Indrani and Sahana standing together, the tension in the air slowly dissipating. As he walked away, she felt a weight lift from her shoulders. She had taken the first step towards her future with Saagar, and she felt more confident and empowered than ever before.

Indrani felt a sense of relief wash over her after the intense encounter between Saagar and Dayanand. It was as if the grey clouds had finally shed their rain, leaving the air clearer and lighter. Without wasting any time, she rushed to her mother, Sumathi, to share what had transpired. As Indrani recounted the episode, Sumathi, Girish, Shreyas, and Pranati listened with rapt attention. They were shocked to learn about the intensity of Saagar's courage, a quality they had all underestimated. Indrani described how Saagar stood his ground while speaking to Dayanand, spoke with unwavering confidence, and boldly declared his intentions.

Sumathi, shaking her head in amazement, said, "I knew Saagar had feelings for Sahana, but I never realized he had such strength and determination. He stood up to Dayanand in a way none of us expected." Girish added, "Saagar showed more courage and clarity than we gave him credit for. It's clear he is deeply committed to Sahana." Pranati, smiling, said, "I always knew there was something special about Saagar, but this... this is incredible. He loves Sahana and is ready to fight for her." Shreyas nodded, agreeing with Pranati. "It's clear Saagar doesn't need our help to elope with Sahana. He's not looking for an escape. He wants to face the situation head-on and earn Dayanand's approval. That's the mark of a true partner."

Sumathi, reflecting on Saagar's words and actions, said, "We should support Saagar and Sahana in their decision. Dayanand might be difficult, but with Saagar's determination and our backing, they can overcome this obstacle." Indrani, feeling a newfound sense of hope, said, "Saagar's confidence has given me the strength to believe that we can get through this. We need to stand by them and ensure Dayanand understands that Sahana's happiness comes first." The family agreed, united in their resolve to support Saagar and Sahana. They understood that while the path ahead might be challenging, Saagar's courage and their collective support would guide them through. As they discussed their next steps, Sumathi said, "Let's talk to Saagar and Sahana, and make sure they know we're behind them. We'll help them navigate this, and together, we can convince Dayanand, too.

On a bright Sunday morning, with newfound confidence and vigor, Sahana walked into Saagar's house. She made her way to his favorite rocking chair and sat down comfortably, waiting for him. A few moments later, Saagar emerged from his room, holding a cup of coffee. He was pleasantly surprised to see Sahana sitting there. A warm smile spread across his face as he admired the new confidence radiating from her. Sahana, catching his look, playfully said, "Won't you invite the guest inside and offer coffee?" Saagar's smile widened, and he responded gently, "The guest became a host in my heart long ago. I'll gladly get coffee for my queen". Sahana blushed deeply, her heart fluttering at his words. Saagar's deep and supportive personality liberated her from fear and stigma, making her feel cherished and strong. As he went to the kitchen to prepare a fresh cup of coffee for her, Sahana looked around his home. It felt warm and welcoming, a reflection of Saagar himself. She realized how much she valued his presence and how much she had grown because of him. Saagar returned with a steaming cup of coffee and handed it to Sahana. She accepted it with a grateful smile, savoring the aroma and the moment. They sat together, enjoying the quiet comfort of each other's company. Sahana broke the silence, "Thank you, Saagar, for everything. You have given me the strength to stand up for myself. "Saagar reached out and gently held her hand. "You had the strength all along, Sahana. I'm just glad I could help you see it. Together, we can face challenges." Sahana's eyes sparkled with determination. "Yes, together." They sat in the rocking chair, gently swaying, as they talked about their future and the steps they would take to build a life together. In that moment, they both knew that their love and mutual respect would guide them through whatever lay ahead, making them stronger as a couple and as individuals.

As she got up to leave, she smiled, "By the way, my parents are going to your native and meet your parents next week to take the proposal further." A stunned Saagar was about to respond when she went out waving a bye.

11. The Second Chance

"Failure is the opportunity to begin again more intelligently."

– Henry Ford

A flustered and visibly agitated Shreyas rushed inside the house to get the car keys. Deepa was about to open her mouth and ask when he informed her, "Vinay has attempted suicide. An ambulance is arriving in 5 minutes. I'm going with them." Deepa was utterly shocked when she heard that Vinay, their childhood neighbor and Shreyas's best friend, had attempted suicide. The news was very unexpected and distressing. She found herself struggling to comprehend it, her mind reeling with disbelief and sorrow. She stood there, trying to process what she had heard. Girish rushed to her side. With a calm and reassuring presence, Girish helped to steady Deepa, offering comforting words and assuring her that they would all come together to support Vinay's parents during this difficult time. Despite the urgency and emotional intensity of the moment, Girish's composure and presence of mind were remarkable, providing a much-needed anchor for Deepa and demonstrating his ability to remain collected and supportive in a crisis.

Vinay and Shreyas shared a deep and enduring friendship, having been best friends since childhood. This close bond between the two boys naturally extended to their families, who, over the years, grew very close. Frequent interactions and shared experiences had solidified almost a familial connection between the households. Deepa had a special fondness for Vinay. She saw him as a soft-spoken, gentle, and obedient child. Someone who was always respectful and considerate. This affectionate regard made Vinay's recent actions even more shocking and heartbreaking for her, as she struggled to reconcile the image of the sweet boy she knew with the distressing news of his suicide attempt.

Shreyas rushed to Vinay's house and got in the ambulance. Deepa and Girish followed him. As the ambulance pulled away, Vinay's mother, Sumitra, was wailing. Deepa rushed to Sumitra and brought her inside. She asked Girish to get the car. They went to the hospital in Girish's car. On their trip to the hospital, all were very quiet; intermittent sobs from Sumitra broke the grim silence. Shreyas and Vinay's father were filling out the forms at the hospital. Shreyas' friends were there and trying to help by calling their acquaintances. They did not want a police complaint. As it is, Vinay's parents were very stressed. Vinay's wife, Hema, was not seen anywhere.

Girish and Deepa approached Nayana, a close cousin of Vinay, who was visiting Vinay's family. Girish asked, "Nayana, if you feel okay, can I know what happened? If I know exactly what happened, I can try my best to figure out how to help." Nayana was sobbing. She was visibly shaken but tried to remain composed, and her voice trembled as she spoke. "Vinay has been struggling with a lot lately, but we didn't realize how bad it was. This morning, we found him unconscious in his room. He had taken many pills. We immediately called for an ambulance. I think he felt overwhelmed and saw no other way out. It's been so hard to see him like this, knowing how much he means to all of us." She paused, taking a deep breath to steady herself. "We're just praying he pulls through. The doctors said getting him to the hospital quickly was crucial."

Initially, the doctors were reluctant to treat a suicide case but started the treatment after a call from a minister who knew the family personally.

Shreyas was in profound distress as he watched Vinay being rushed into the ICU, his friend's critical condition shaking him to his core. Known for being a typically withdrawn person who seldom offered help unless explicitly asked, Shreyas displayed an uncharacteristic determination and concern. He refused to leave the hospital, insisting on staying until he was assured of Vinay's stability. This unexpected display of commitment and emotional involvement did not go unnoticed. Pranati, observing from a distance, was struck by the dramatic change in Shreyas. She saw how the gravity of Vinay's situation had drawn out a depth of care and steadfastness in Shreyas that she had never seen before—deeply loyal and compassionate in times of crisis.

Over time, Vinay's condition gradually stabilized. An intense worry had gripped his parents, Sumitra and Ganesh. It began to ease as they saw signs of improvement in their son. The doctor informed them that Vinay could soon be discharged, but recommended that he attend counseling sessions with a psychologist to aid in his recovery. Girish and Deepa provided reassurance and support. They promised to be there for Vinay and his family through the recovery. They were committed to helping Vinay heal and regain his physical and emotional strength.

Deepa and Girish observed that, through the hospital stay, Vinay's wife, Hema, was missing from the scene. Girish was wondering how to ask about Hema without embarrassing Sumitra and Ganesh. One Friday afternoon, Deepa called Sumitra and told her, "Sumitra, today I am cooking lunch for everyone. Please rest. We will all have food at your place.".

Sumitra truly felt grateful: "I don't have words to thank you and your family, Deepa, for the unsolicited support." Deepa said, "We are like family, Sumitra. It is give-and-take. Even I can't forget all the selfless help you have offered when I was in need. The way you have taken care of my kids when they were ill and when I was stuck in the office for extended hours was a big help. Now is not the time to be formal. Expect me there in 10 minutes. It's been ages since we listened to music on good old Sundays. Why can't we listen to the "aap ki farmaaish" program on Vividbharati radio station and have lunch?" Sumitra was happy and invited them warmly.

Deepa, Sumitra, Girish, and Ganesh had lunch together. Girish and Ganesh went out, and while going, Ganesh said, "Sumitra, we will meet a lawyer, go for a coffee, and be back home." Deepa was puzzled when he mentioned the lawyer. After they left, Sumitra opened. "Deepa, so many things happened so suddenly in our lives!" Deepa said, "See, we must have friends and family on the speed dial list. Of late, we haven't shared much of our pain and happiness. But the bond has remained unchanged. Please vent if you have heaviness inside you. Why make it a volcano inside? What is happening, Sumitra? Where is Hema? Is there any problem with Vinay's marriage?" Sumitra started sobbing. With tears in her eyes, she said, "Vinay had not shared his problems with anyone, not even with us or his sister Vinutha. Though Vinutha stays in America, she is always a second mother to him, and he could have opened up to her at least or Shreyas, his best friend."

"Deepa, you know Vinay's wedding was a surprise for all, including us. I heard about this girl, Hema, from one of our relatives. Her family isn't wealthy—her mother has worked tirelessly to raise her, especially since her father's health forced him to stop working years ago. Despite their hardships, Hema had completed her education and was working. When I heard her story, Deepa, I couldn't help but feel deeply moved. I thought that someone who had faced such challenges early in her life would be humble and willing to adapt to our family. Ganesh, of course, wanted to check into their background thoroughly. But I was so swept up by the idea of bringing this girl into our lives. I imagined her as the obedient daughter-in-law who would respect and listen to us. Perhaps my emotions had the upper hand, creating the narrative that I was offering a better life to a deserving, struggling girl. Vinay, on the other hand, was understandably puzzled. He assumed we must have thoroughly vetted this girl and her family before considering her for him. But Vinay's marriage was a failure!"

"Deepa, as you know, I have always been a bit naive about judging people. I genuinely believe that most people have good intentions, and I've never been wary of anyone. I believed that bad people only existed in movies. It's hard for me to imagine anyone wanting to cause harm. Life has been kind to us; it's been smooth sailing. Our faith in God is strong, and we are grateful that our children have grown up with the right values. Our daughter's wedding happened without a hitch, and we were overjoyed when she started her own family, blessed with children and a loving home. For us, Deepa, it's about cherishing these simple blessings and trusting in the goodness of people." Deepa held her hands and said, "Sumitra, nothing happened to Vinay. It is a passing cloud. The sun will shine. Goodness pays, and bright days will come. Cheer up."

That night, while having dinner, Deepa narrated what Sumitra shared. Girish listened to it calmly and said, "We wrongly associate values with financial status and struggle. My own experience does not agree that anyone who has struggled will automatically be virtuous. I've seen cases where people feel entitled to special treatment because they have suffered. Also, if someone extends help, the demands grow. Many have an attitude of anyway, they are doing, let me extract as much as possible." Sumathi also agreed that Sumitra was not the best judge of character.

Sumathi recalled, "Vinay's wedding was six months after our Shreyas', right?" Pranati pitched in, "Yes, Ajji. Remember, Sumitra Aunty had taken me shopping for Hema's saree." Pranati continued sharing with all, especially Deepa, "Amma, we were shopping for sarees, and I noticed how her eyes would light up at the sight of the many options. Despite not speaking much, when others suggested a saree for her, she would politely decline, saying it wouldn't suit her color or personality. I started observing closely. By the end of the shopping spree, Sumitra Aunty had spent almost double her planned budget, and Hema ended up with the most expensive sarees. Sumitra Aunty didn't realize what had happened; she thought Hema had valid reasons for her choices. I couldn't help but feel that Hema might not be exactly how Sumitra aunty perceives her to be. There seems to be a disconnect, especially concerning our cultural values. I was skeptical about getting close to her after seeing her behavior."

Deepa had not heard Pranati say anything about anyone. She was happy that Pranati had started checking people before letting them into their homes. So far, Deepa had protected Pranati from the hassles of social issues in the family. Maybe it was time for Pranati to see the reality. Deepa decided not to give her opinion and let Pranati connect the dots to understand the gravity of the situation. Following Pranati's experience, to all their surprise, Shreyas, who is usually an introvert opened up!

"I spoke to Vinay, and this is what I gathered. As destiny ordained, no caution from anyone worked. Ganesh and Sumitra hosted the wedding almost fully, and Hema entered their home. The initial few months were all dreamy. Hema was slowly taking over the house. She agreed to whatever Sumitra Aunty said. Vinay was super happy with his obedient wife. After 3 months, she asked Vinay for some money. Her father's condition was not very good, and he needed some medical procedures. Vinay did not ask much for details. By then, trust was building. He did not ask how much it would cost but gave her a large amount. She may need money for post-operation care. Her mother was also quiet and would not speak much. Vinay's surmised struggles have made them wary.

In the next few months, the demand for money increased. It was a debt because of her father's condition. She had stated that the interest was growing on earlier debts. Vinay got her first taste of deception when she called him and said someone would come over to collect cash at his office and give him the amount. Vinay asked who he was and why he should pay. She said it was one of the creditors from whom they had borrowed money. If they did not pay, he threatened that he would come home and create a scene. She was worried that his parents were respectful and did not want a scene at home. A totally confused Vinay came down and paid the person.

This story kept repeating. Vinay was seeing his savings reach almost zero. He had tried talking to her about the entire debt. She was elusive. She would give some lists that could not be verified. These were not bank loans. The relative who had told the sob story was spilling other things after marriage. There were many women in their locality involved in chit-funding. There were lots of financial transactions. Vinay was not able to track any of them. When questioned, she would start sobbing, saying that she had struggled and that even after marriage, no one understood her.

Vinay's stress levels were mounting exponentially. He would not know when anyone would appear to ask for what amount. He did not want to trouble his father, as he was growing old. His sister was away. He had thought of confiding in me many times. But then, it felt awkward discussing his wife and her ways with his dear friend.

Hema got bolder by the day and started getting her chit-fund friend's home. They would have kitty parties. Sumitra Aunty and Ganesh Uncle were lost. What was she up to? Even their naïve minds could comprehend that things were not okay. The women whom Hema used to call home did not look cultured and pious. Many were loud, constantly discussing money. Hema did not bother to give them an explanation. She knew they were soft targets who valued their respect and honor enough to blackmail them into remaining quiet. Sumitra Aunty was getting sick. She was blaming herself fully for spoiling her son's life. Ganesh Uncle blamed himself for not checking Hema's background fully. Vinay was not thinking anymore. He seemed drained of all spirit and presence.

The last straw was when rowdy-looking goons entered their home and threatened his parents to part with money. They had complied, but he could not handle the stress anymore. He locked himself in and attempted suicide." Shreyas continued, "I asked him, "What have you thought of for the future?" Vinay said, "I don't know. I need professional help, a lawyer." I told Vinay's decision to Appa. He and Ganesh Uncle had gone to meet Appa's lawyer friend today. Appa, I hope Vinay gets an understanding life partner and continues with his life without bitterness. His parents' health is not good."

Girish replied, "Shreyas, I'm not for divorce, but when trust and integrity are lost in a marriage, there's no point in trying to hold on. Without these foundations, the relationship becomes irreparable. Vinay needs to understand and think about moving forward." Girish clarified, "Going through a tough marriage isn't a failure; it's a chance to learn and grow. I urge Vinay to use his intellect and make decisions based on reason, not just emotions. We need to support Vinay. Shreyas, help him make choices that lead to his happiness and well-being."

Girish was observing Shreyas try to help his friend. A normally non-interfering Shreyas was determined to see his friend sort out the mess. The divorce was not smooth. Hema was a profound actress. She and her relatives extracted enough money from Vinay's family before letting them go. Vinay was wary of life itself.

Shreyas had taken him on a trek for a week after his divorce. The quiet mountains had started the healing process.

Shreyas suggested, "Guys, why don't we take Vinay's family to the temple pooja at our native place? They could use a break; they've been through so much." Sumathi, Deepa, and Girish immediately nodded in agreement. They all understood the importance of providing support and a change of scenery for Vinay's family during such trying times. They were hoping Vinay's family would get some relief and comfort.

That night, post-dinner, Shreyas and Pranati went to the terrace and enjoyed the sight of the star-studded night sky. It was serene, and the stars were more evident as it was a new moon. Shreyas commented, "The sky looks dull without a moon." Pranati said, "Sometimes the absence of the moon is needed to view the bright stars!" Shreyas smiled and said, "Always, you will come up with some counterstatements!" Pranati said, "Dexterity, easy flow, and being open to options make life easy. If we become rigid, we fail to see beauty in anything, Shreyas." Shreyas said, "What you say is true, Pranati. I think that's why you are much more accommodating than I!"

Pranati said, "Shreyas, can I ask something?" Shreyas smiled at Pranati and said, "I know the question is a formality. Even if I say no, you will still make your suggestion. Please go ahead." Pranati said, "How old is Shambhavi?" Shreyas asked, "Which Shambhavi?". "That priest Dattu Shastry's daughter, that pretty girl, who is a Sanskrit scholar," Shreyas said, "She is three years younger than me; she must be 25 now. Why did she come in between us at this time?" Pranati said, "I just thought that she would be a perfect match for our Vinay. By looks as well as by their thoughts." Shreyas was stunned. "Oh my God! I think even Bollywood directors take time to decide the heroes and heroines for their movies. But you are a bullet train, much faster!" Pranati said, "Last time, after our wedding, when we went to Dattu Shastry's house, I got to spend more than an hour with Shambhavi. I felt she was a very thoughtful and beautiful girl. A deep person. While Appa told you to help Vinay move on, suddenly she flashed in my mind." Shreyas thought, "Actually, not a bad idea." He said, "Let us not rush. First, talk to Appa and Amma. They can suggest whether it is wise to proceed. Hats off to your brain-wiring, Pranati! I thought only dreams and fantasies nested in your brains. I never knew even great ideas were there." Pranati grinned and said, "Yes, how I wish great ideas had flashed when I was dating you; I would not have married you." Shreyas was taken aback. Pranati giggled and called Shreyas, "Mr. Tubelight, please come down; tomorrow we have to get ready early for the temple."

Pranati was a bubbly, impulsive girl and could not hold this exciting idea in her for long. When they came down from the terrace, Sumathi was fast asleep, and Girish and Deepa were about to retire to bed. Pranati knocked on Deepa's door and called Deepa and Girish. Deepa came out and said, "It's so late. You guys have not slept yet? Is everything alright?" Shreyas said, "Your daughter-in-law has a brilliant idea, Amma." Deepa was excited to listen. Pranati suggested the proposal of Shambhavi to Vinay. Deepa and Girish were stunned. Girish said, "Actually, before Vinay's wedding, when Dattu Shastry had asked me to look for a groom for Shambhavi, I had Vinay in mind. But he was already engaged to Hema. So, I thought destiny had different plans and dropped it."

Deepa said, "This is a little sensitive now. We can't rush. Anyway, tomorrow, we can discuss it with Dattu

Shastry and later with Vinay. Shreyas, counsel Vinay that he needs to move on in life." The drive to the temple was around two and a half hours. Shreyas had strictly warned Pranati not to talk about Shambhavi, obviously, to Vinay. He knew that secrets could slip easily out of her. On the way, Girish started, "Ganesh, I want you to meet the priest, Dattu Shastry, there. He is a kind, scholarly gentleman. He has taken over the temple from his father and trained his children to take over from him. He is leading a peaceful life. They have land in the village." Shreyas felt that Girish was smarter than all. He was laying the foundation for the proposal with Ganesh Uncle. Pranati and Shreyas exchanged smiles, as the same thing was running through her mind too!

The trip to Shreyas' native temple, nestled on a serene mountaintop, was a much-needed escape for Vinay and his family. The tranquility of the surroundings, with the fresh mountain air and the gentle sounds of nature, helped lift the heavy mood weighing on Vinay's heart. As they walked through the temple grounds, Vinay felt a sense of peace and hope begin to blossom within him. The families enjoyed the spiritual solace and serenity, feeling an inexplicable calm descend over them. After the temple visit, they were warmly welcomed to the home of the priest, Dattu Shastry, where they savored the simple yet delicious food and genuine hospitality. Vinay was particularly struck by the ambiance of the Shastry's ancestral home, filled with beautiful paintings and shelves lined with philosophical books. He met Shambhavi, Dattu

Shastry's daughter, whose appearance and choices left a deep impression on him. Her simplicity, radiant smile, and profound depth made her a captivating presence. The glimpses of her life, her thoughtful choices in books, and her art on the walls spoke volumes about her rich inner world. It was a moment of unexpected revelation for Vinay, a small spark of hope and connection amid his turmoil.

Post-lunch, Sumitra and Ganesh shared their bitter experience with Dattu Shastry, as he was also an astrologer, and they wanted him to foresee Vinay's future. The priest empathized with them and sighed, "Humans can live such a wonderful life. Alas, even when God gives abundantly, greed blinds us." He said he would let Deepa know if he had any good proposals. Just then, his daughter, Shambavi, entered. Pranati was getting excited. Why didn't Deepa propose Shambavi and Vinay's match? She pulled Girish aside and asked him. He smiled and said, "Pranati, we cannot move forward without understanding the aspirations of both families." Girish continued, "The priest is a wise man. He has seen all kinds of people come to the temple for their own reasons. He will assess the situation and discuss it with his family—especially his daughter. If they agree, Sumitra and Ganesh will hear from them."

Pranati had learned a valuable lesson. Imagination can run wild. She was already participating in Vinay and Shambavi's wedding in the temple. But Girish was right, as usual. She cannot assume anything about others. She made a note in her mind. As they started back, there was a glimmer of hope in Sumitra's eyes. Deepa smiled reassuringly at her. Pranati was seeing a graceful exchange of hope between women without any words being spoken. She was thinking, "When will I learn this grace?"

Girish confirmed to Ganesh, "Whenever I have come to this temple, I have never gone empty-handed. I feel there is some divine grace here. Ganesh, I am sure everything will be okay." They reached home by night, and there was a letter in Ganesh's house post box. It was the divorce approval from the court. Sumitra took a deep sigh and felt a bit relieved. She said," Vinay, it was a bitter dream. Please forget it."

That same night, at his house, Dattu Shastry took Vinay's horoscope and checked for his prospects. With his profound astrological insight, he made some mental calculations and immediately took out Shambhavi's horoscope. He saw that those two matched perfectly and were compatible for marriage. As per astrology, he saw charts blend harmoniously. He immediately called his wife, Lakshmi, and shared this observation. Despite his positive evaluation, his wife, Lakshmi, was apprehensive. Her concern stemmed from Vinay being a divorcee. Should they consider a divorcee for their only daughter?

In response to Lakshmi's concerns, Dattu Shastry suggested conducting a thorough background check on Vinay and his family. In this regard, Dattu Shastry and Lakshmi came down to Bengaluru and went to Girish's house. At Girish's house, all were very glad to host them. Deepa and Sumathi prepared a satvik meal for them, and post-dinner, Dattu Shastry spoke to Girish about his observation. Girish was excited. When a wish comes true, there is no boundary to happiness! But Dattu Shastry said he needs to know completely about Vinay as it is a matter of his daughter's future, and he can't make any decision in haste. Girish said, "Definitely, what you say is true. You can get information about Vinay from his friends, neighbors, and colleagues." Dattu said, "They are not foolproof. Sometimes, there is a lot of disparity between what a person appears to others and what he is." Girish understood that something was on Dattu Shastry's mind.

Dattu Shastry was a man of wisdom and wit. He valued not just intelligence but also the qualities of a true family leader. Dattu said, "To ensure that Vinay is the perfect match for my daughter, I have devised a series of intricate scenarios to test Vinay's resourcefulness, protective instincts, and decision-making skills. Now I don't want Vinay to know this. Just call Shreyas, Vinay, and other friends; casually, I will ask them and evaluate Vinay.".

Girish was amazed. "Very impressive indeed!" Dattu grinned. "This should be confidential. Between you and me!". Girish nodded and assured him that it would be a secret. Girish called Shreyas and asked him to call Vinay and his parents to meet Dattu Shastry and his wife. Post-dinner, they came over for a visit. Vinay's eyes were silently searching Shambhavi when Sumati interrupted, "Dattu, you must bring Shambhavi home next time you come." The ripple of excitement in Vinay's heart diffused as he listened to that conversation. Dattu's laser eyes were on Vinay and his parents, though he never made it look evident. He was observing the humble, homely nature of Sumitra and Ganesh.

In the living room, Pranati, Shreyas, and Vinay were watching a movie. Casually, Dattu and Girish came and sat on the sofa, and Dattu asked, "So what are you watching?" Shreyas replied," It's an old classic love story. Dattu uncle, I will change the channel if you want to watch any other program." Dattu said, "No that's okay, you people carry on with the movie. But since you mentioned a love story, I want to tell you youngsters something." Immediately, all three paused the movie and paid attention to Dattu uncle. He addressed Shreyas, Pranati, and Vinay, "It is easy to say you love someone, but love is also about protection and leadership. Just for fun, I want to give you certain tricky situations. Let's see, if you were in this position, how you would handle each situation. Ready?". They got excited.

Vinay, Shreyas, and Pranati smirked with determination. "Dattu uncle, we are ready." Dattu set the stage: "You must answer one after the other. First, Vinay, I want to hear from you! Now let me explain this intruder's incident. Imagine it's late at night, and you hear a noise downstairs. Your wife and the kids are asleep. What do you do?" Vinay didn't hesitate. "First, I will check that my wife and the kids are safe and secure in a room, locking them in if necessary. Then, I grab the nearest item for self-defense, like a heavy lamp, and cautiously investigate. If it's an intruder, I call the authorities immediately and try to confront him."

Dattu (nodding, impressed): "Good. Always put family safety first while managing threats." Dattu leans forward, "Now let me try to bring up the financial dilemma. Suppose you discover that, due to a mix-up, your bank account is overdrawn, and you have bills to pay. What would you do?". For a while, Vinay was lost; his past bitter experiences with Hema flashed before his eyes. Suddenly, Shreyas caught his pulse, lightened the air, and cheered Vinay. "Vinay, you need to answer all the questions. Later, it will be passed to us! Come on, answer. Do not delay." Vinay came back to his senses and thought carefully: "I would first inform my wife to make sure she checks my bank details. Then, I'd contact the bank to rectify the mistake and explain the situation to our creditors. Meanwhile, we would cut down on unnecessary expenses and use the emergency funds. It's crucial to communicate openly and maintain calm. Strategic actions are needed during financial turbulence. "Dattu (smiling): "Excellent. Transparency and calm problem-solving are key."

Dattu continued, "The next scenario is about health. Imagine one of your children falling seriously ill during a vacation in a foreign country. Medical facilities are far away, and the situation is dire. What do you do?" Vinay responded with concern: "First, I would use any available means to contact the local medical services and get immediate assistance. If necessary, I'd drive or carry the child to the nearest facility. I'd also ensure we have a travel health insurance plan before traveling to handle such emergencies. Keeping calm and acting swiftly is vital to safeguarding my child's health." Dattu (nodding approvingly): "Swift action and preparation—well done."

Dattu's eyes twinkled. Next, let me throw an emotional challenge: "Imagine your wife is stressed out from work and family responsibilities. She feels overwhelmed. How do you support her?" Vinay answers tenderly: "I'd take on more household responsibilities to lighten her load, or suggest extra paid help, and arrange a special evening to help her relax, perhaps a nice dinner or a weekend getaway. Most importantly, I'd listen to her concerns, reassuring her that we're a team and we will get through tough times together." Dattu (grinning widely): "Compassion and partnership are essential for a strong marriage." Dattu says the final scenario is a community crisis. "Your neighborhood faces a crisis, like a natural disaster. As a husband and a community member, what steps do you take to ensure safety and cooperation among neighbors?"

Vinay responded confidently: "First, I assess the situation. I'd take steps to keep my family safe. Leadership isn't just about my family; it's about extending that care to the community. I'd gather essential supplies and coordinate with neighbors to create a support system, ensuring everyone had what they needed. Establishing a communication network and a plan for emergencies is crucial." Dattu (clapping): "Bravo, Vinay. Leadership, empathy, and strategic thinking—qualities of a true family leader." Later, he asked the same questions to Shreyas and Pranati, ensuring Vinay's interview was not obvious.

Dattu Shastry felt very impressed, and in his heart, he had a nod of approval and welcomed Vinay into the family. The scenarios weren't just about testing intelligence but evaluating the qualities that make a reliable, caring, and strong leader of a family. After Vinay's family took leave, Dattu Shastry called Girish and told him, "I do not need any other background verification. He has passed my acid test!" Girish felt very happy. Dattu continued, "Now the person who must decide is Shambhavi. Let us see what her opinion is. That's the final verdict, and only that is important. All these are preliminary tests."

Dattu and Lakshmi went back to their temple home. That night, Dattu Shastry called and spoke to Shambhavi. He narrated the questionnaire session he conducted and explained how he was impressed with Vinay's answer. He said, "Shambhavi, Vinay is a potential match; based on astrological compatibility and Vinay's personal qualities, I can vouch for that. I know he had a terrible, bitter experience with his first marriage. But it's fate. I feel he has good character and values, and I feel strongly that he is aligned with your aspirations and beliefs."

Dattu Shastry, scholarly and knowledgeable, presented his observations thoughtfully, highlighting Vinay's achievements, gentlemanly nature, and respectful behavior during their interactions. He discussed how Vinay's background and experiences complemented Shambhavi's personality and life goals.

Shambhavi, being thoughtful and understanding, listened to her father's perspective with respect. She reflected on her own interactions with Vinay, recalling moments that showed his kindness, intelligence, and sincerity. These qualities resonated with her, reinforcing her father's assessment that Vinay was indeed a suitable match. Shambhavi gracefully accepted the proposal as she realized that Vinay possessed the qualities she valued in a life partner. Her acceptance was a blend of trust in her father's judgment and her own positive impressions of Vinay, leading to a decision rooted in both practicality and genuine connection.

One Sunday morning, Vinay had dropped by Shreyas's home. Shreyas, Pranati, and Vinay were having a heated debate about current politics. Girish had successfully kept Dattu's intent of testing Vinay a top secret! Girish came to the living room and interrupted them. "Vinay, I wanted to call you. It is good that you are here. Dattu Shastry had called. They are looking for a proposal for his daughter, Shambhavi. Can I suggest yours?" Vinay was blank. Pranati's imagination of the Vinay Shambhavi marriage in the temple was coming true! Vinay excused himself from there after saying that he would revert after speaking to his parents.

With a sense of sincerity and determination, Vinay expressed his intentions regarding Shambhavi to his parents. He began by acknowledging their potential concerns, and if they had no objections, he would propose to Shambhavi. With Hema, he was not clear about his life partner. But now he had given it enough thought. Vinay underscored his desire for a meaningful life. He communicated his acceptance of Shambhavi as a life partner, highlighting his readiness and commitment to embark on a new chapter of his life with someone who could resonate deeply with him.

The coming weekend, Shreyas and Vinay's families went to Dattu Shastry's house to talk about the proposal, and the marriage was fixed. Vinay, a shy person, expressed to Pranati, "Pranati, I need to talk to Shambhavi before the elders finalize it on cards. Can you help?" Pranati giggled. "Mr. Passenger train. You are so slow. I told Shambhavi on your behalf that you will meet her in the temple in the evening." Vinay was awestruck at Pranati's fast reflex! He said, "Thanks a lot."

The sunset over the serene mountaintop had cast a gentle glow on the temple premises. Shambhavi appeared like a vision, draped in a delicate baby-pink cotton saree. Her graceful movements as she walked towards Vinay captivated him instantly. Vinay's heart skipped a beat as he beheld her elegance, a sensation he had never experienced. Her presence seemed to illuminate the tranquil surroundings, her every step exuding poise and charm. The gentle sway of her saree and the soft glow of the evening light reflecting on her features all added to the enchanting moment. Vinay was mesmerized by Shambhavi's beauty and grace, a sight that filled his heart with admiration and a deep sense of joy.

Vinay felt comfortable sharing a personal part of his life with Shambhavi. Sitting together in the peaceful ambiance, he spoke at length about his past, revealing that he was a divorcee who had faced hardships in his previous marriage. He expressed deep gratitude to Shambhavi for accepting his proposal. Looking into her eyes, he assured her of his commitment to being a devoted husband and a lifelong friend. He promised to honour their relationship with understanding and support, seeking to build a loving and meaningful partnership rooted in mutual respect and companionship. Vinay's words carried a sincerity that resonated with the tranquil surroundings, creating a moment of profound connection and openness between them.

Vinay and Shambhavi's wedding was a serene and blissful affair held at the temple, surrounded by the peaceful ambiance of the temple town. The setting was simple yet filled with profound meaning, with elders and Vedic scholars in attendance, lending an air of sanctity to the occasion. The rituals were conducted with reverence, with each step guided by tradition and the blessings of those present. The presence of Girish's family added to the joyous atmosphere. In the temple, the couple exchanged vows and promises; their union symbolized not a mere marriage, but the merging of two souls in harmony. The simplicity of the ceremony highlighted the essence of their commitment and love, making it a memorable day of new beginnings and heartfelt blessings from all who gathered to witness their union.

12. Rising to a Role

*"The key to teamwork is to learn a role, accept a role,
and strive to become excellent playing it."*

– Pat Riley

Girish was busy cleaning the outhouse to rent out. He saw Pranati leave the house alone. Pranati and Shreyas were expecting a baby soon. Girish was uncomfortable that Pranati was driving alone. Before he could call her, he saw her get into the car and drive away. He came in hastily and asked Shreyas. "Where did Pranati go, and why did she go alone?" Shreyas looked up. "Appa, she has gone to a function. It is at her friend's house. Maybe a thirty-minute drive." Girish looked concerned. Shreyas heard him tell Deepa, "Traffic is increasing on this route. It is about to rain as well. I wish one of us had dropped her." Shreyas felt it was not a big deal.

He said, "Appa, she has been driving for years. Yes, her condition at present is not conducive to driving. But she has no major issues, and didn't the doctor say she had to be active?", saying this, Shreyas started hurrying up as it was getting late for his photography session. These days, he was passionate about photography and wanted to excel. He loved the lighting, perfect angles, and moving objects. A wonderful world had opened up for him. His weekends were almost entirely consumed by photography, attending classes, and venturing to find the perfect shots.

However, this intense focus on his new hobby was causing Shreyas to slip away from his responsibilities at home. This was particularly concerning given that he and Pranati were expecting a child. Despite the impending arrival of their baby, Shreyas was neglecting important tasks and duties at home. Pranati, who needed his support more than ever, was left to manage things by herself. Shreyas' preoccupation with photography meant he was increasingly absent from the home front, not preparing for their growing family or providing the emotional and practical support that Pranati needed during this critical time. Girish, Deepa, and now Pranati together ensured that things ran efficiently. He had made financial investments, and he felt that was enough. He was now free to pursue his passion fully.

This coming Sunday, Pranati has a regular checkup scheduled. Shreyas had promised to accompany her, but a last-minute opportunity to learn from a master photographer in his domain had arisen. Not wanting to miss this chance, Shreyas hesitantly asked Pranati if it would be okay for him to skip the appointment. She was disappointed but said she would go with Deepa. Shreyas failed to notice the disappointment on her face. When Girish inquired about his plans, Shreyas casually mentioned that Deepa would join Pranati instead. Sensing Shreyas' detachment, Girish probed further: "Well, don't you want to know how things are going? Are there any concerns? What does Pranati need?" Caught off guard, Shreyas replied, "She seems to be fine with me going." Feeling a pang of guilt, he mumbled something about getting late and quickly left for his photography session, leaving Girish's words echoing in his mind. Deepa accompanied Pranati to her gynaecologist check-up. The doctor confirmed that everything was normal, bringing a sense of relief to Pranati. On the way back home, Deepa sensed Pranati's lingering disappointment. She decided to share her own experiences. "Pranati, do you know?" Deepa began gently. "I had a very demanding job when I was carrying Shreyas. Balancing work and pregnancy was tough, and I often felt overwhelmed."

Pranati listened attentively as Deepa continued, "At times, I wished I could slow down and savour the experience. These moments of carrying your baby, feeling those first kicks, and nurturing a life inside you are incredibly special and fleeting. Once they're gone, you can't get them back." Deepa paused, giving Pranati a warm smile. "Don't get caught up in the rat race, my dear. It's important to enjoy this beautiful phase of your life. Take time to bond with your baby, to cherish the small joys, and to take care of yourself. Work and other passions will always be there, but this journey of motherhood is unique. "Pranati nodded, absorbing Deepa's words. "Thank you, Amma. I needed to hear that." Deepa squeezed her hand reassuringly. "You're doing great, Pranati. Enjoy every moment, and don't be afraid to ask for help. Slow down when you need to. It's all part of the journey."

Girish enjoyed spending his time in the outhouse after Saagar moved out. He was immersing himself in his spiritual studies. He assumed that Shreyas would naturally take over the responsibilities around the house in his absence. However, this assumption proved incorrect. The burden was increasingly falling on Deepa and Pranati. He observed and wondered how this would play out in the long run. Girish's mind was in turmoil. He realized that while he was focused on his spiritual journey, he also needed to ensure that Shreyas stepped into his role as the man of the house and father. Girish contemplated, "How do I transition from being the primary caretaker to a guiding elder? How can I support my family during this transition?"

One evening, Girish decided to have a heart-to-heart conversation with Shreyas. He found him in the living room, editing some of his recent photographs. "Shreyas, can we talk for a moment?" Girish asked, his tone serious yet gentle. "Sure, Dad. What's on your mind?" Shreyas asked, sensing the seriousness of the tone. Girish took a deep breath and continued,

"I've been thinking a lot about our family and shared responsibilities. After Saagar left , I'm spending more time on my spiritual studies in the outhouse. I had assumed you'd pick up the slack. But I realized I haven't been fair to you, Pranati, and Deepa." Shreyas looked down, feeling a mix of guilt and confusion." I know you're passionate about photography. I admire your dedication." Girish continued, "But Pranati needs you now more than ever, especially with the baby on the way. This is a crucial time for both of you, and you need to be there for her, emotionally and practically." Shreyas nodded slowly. "I understand, Dad. I've been so caught up in my world that I didn't see how much Pranati and Mom needed me." Girish placed a reassuring hand on his son's shoulder. "It's not too late, Shreyas. You can still make a difference. Start by being present for Pranati, attending her check-ups, and helping at home. Show her that she has all the support."

Shreyas felt a wave of determination wash over him. "You're right, Dad. I'll do better. I'll be there for Pranati and for you and Mom." Girish smiled, feeling a sense of relief. "That's all I ask, son. We're a family, and we need to support each other. I'll always be here to guide you, but it's time for you to step into your role as a husband and soon-to-be father." With that, Shreyas felt a renewed sense of purpose. He knew the journey ahead would require balance and sacrifice, but he was ready to embrace his responsibilities and be the partner and father his family needed. In the afternoon, Deepa joined Girish in the outhouse for coffee. Girish was deep in thought, still grappling with his concerns about Shreyas. As they sat down, he narrated the recent instances that had troubled him, emphasizing how he felt Shreyas was shirking his responsibilities. Deepa listened patiently before offering her perspective. "I think you are overreacting, Girish. Right now, Shreyas is busy pursuing something close to his heart. Once the initial excitement dies down, he'll likely be his usual self." Girish shook his head, his worry evident. "What if the excitement remains? Right now, photography has his heart. Let's assume he will get bored in a few months. From what I see, this isn't just a hobby; it's his passion. Any passionate person will prioritize their passion over everything else." Deepa sighed, understanding the depth of Girish's concern. "Even if he does outgrow this particular passion, his nature suggests he'll find something else to throw himself into. Deepa, think about the scenario where Pranati will end up shouldering most of the responsibilities at home. Yesterday, you gave her the grocery list, and she ordered online. Shreyas excused himself by saying, The maids take care of things. But someone has to oversee them." Girish continued, his voice tinged with frustration. "At this rate, it will be Pranati overseeing everything, and she'll also have a small baby to look after. Even if we pitch in, this is not right." Deepa placed her hand on Girish's arm, soothing his anxiety. "I understand your concerns, Girish. But perhaps instead of assuming the worst, we could try to guide Shreyas without stifling his passion. You already had an open conversation with him. He will learn to balance his interests and responsibilities." Girish nodded slowly, considering her words. "You're right, Deepa. I had an open conversation. But we also must help him understand how his roles as a supportive husband and soon-to-be father are crucial. We can support him, but he needs to step up." Deepa smiled gently. "Let's approach this with empathy. Shreyas might not fully realize the impact of his role shift yet. If we help him see things from Pranati's perspective and ours, he might find the balance sooner."

Deepa looked forward to helping raise their grandchild when Pranati went to the office. She had not even considered Shreyas's role as father. She walked back, still thinking about what Girish had said. After Sumathi passed on, she saw Girish gradually withdraw. At first, she thought it was because of the deep grief he felt, having loved his mother dearly. Sumathi had lived with them for a long time, even seeing her grandchildren marry. Deepa was missing Sumathi, but Pranati's needs had kept her busy. Sumathi would be so happy to hold her great-grandchild. Deepa sighed. These days, she had no one at home to express her thoughts and emotions. Pranati was way too young. When it came to Shreyas, the protective mother in her always took over, making it difficult to have frank conversations. Laya, her other daughter, was busy building her own home after marriage, and Deepa didn't want to burden her with her worries. Pranati was scheduled to go to her mother's home in a few weeks and would return after a few months with the baby. The entire family eagerly awaited the arrival of the new baby. Deepa's mind was in turmoil, a mix of concern, dreams, and prayers for a safe delivery. She had told Pranati's mother, Sudha, to call her for anything. Sudha was getting anxious about handling everything by herself during Pranati's delivery. Deepa wanted to be a support system for Sudha. Deepa recalled how her mother and mother-in-law worked in tandem to help her during her pregnancy, and tears of gratitude rolled down her face.

Shreyas would be gone on weekends chasing some tiger or exotic bird. Pranati was lost in her world; the physical demands of pregnancy left her tired and eager to meet their baby. Shreyas started planning a longer photography trip with his friends. Pranati would be away, and this was the right time for his hobby. He dreamed of spending a few weeks in Assam, or even Africa. His dreams were now full of wild elephants and boars. Though he was concerned for Pranati, he thought his parents and her parents would be there for her and the baby. He was needed only when they needed a driver. After all, this was his first experience with a baby, and he felt unprepared. Pranati, on the other hand, was growing increasingly tired and emotionally drained. The anticipation of the baby's arrival was both exciting and overwhelming. She needed Shreyas's support more than ever, but he seemed distant, wrapped up in his pursuits.

After Pranati left for her mother's place, Shreyas told Girish and Deepa that he wanted to go on a two-week trip to Africa. Girish and Deepa were aghast. Deepa blurted, "What? Your baby is due anytime. Don't you want to be around to welcome the child?". Shreyas said, "The doctor has said it will take at least

3 weeks for the baby to arrive. I've planned my trip based on this date. I'll be back a week before then." Deepa was getting angry by then. "How does the doctor know it will be exactly 3 weeks? A baby can arrive any time after nine months. Also, Pranati will want you around when she is going through the most important period of her life. It is not enough that you call her from afar. Have you checked what she wants now?" Shreyas was lost. His passion had not let him inquire much about her, even when she was here. Deepa would insist, and he had taken her wherever she wanted to go and bought her whatever she felt like buying or eating. But, on his own, he had not done anything from his heart. He felt guilty. He said, "I'll cancel this trip and plan for after the baby is born.". Deepa shouted, "Not until the baby is at least 6 months old. Even then, I'm not for you going far with a small child at home. I hope you will realize your new role and its responsibilities in 6 months." Girish smiled at Deepa. She had done the right thing. Shreyas started visiting Pranati more often. He felt sorry for her, as she struggled to manage her heavy weight every day. He understood she was getting tired quickly. Sudha was relieved to see Shreyas take over when he visited them. Any small change in Pranati, and she would become anxious. The baby arrived on time. It was a baby boy. The family was overjoyed and started preparations to welcome Pranati and the baby home.

Shreyas would not leave the side of the baby. He was mesmerized by the delicate entity in front of him. He wanted to shield the child from all harm. He wanted to provide the best of the best. Pranati had not seen this caring side of Shreyas. He had a thousand plans running through his head for the future education of his child. Pranati would listen for some time and doze off. She had months to recover from delivering the magic. Girish was noticing the change in Shreyas. One afternoon, he casually asked Deepa, "What do you say we shift to the outhouse?" She asked, "Like all of us? Are you planning any repairs before Pranati returns?" He carefully chose his words: "No, just the two of us moving. Shreyas's family is growing. They will need space." Deepa said, "In the same house, we raised two children with elders. Why do you think we cannot do it now?" Girish was at a loss for words. He asked her to think about it. He wanted Shreyas to rise to the role of a father. With them around, he might not rise to his role soon enough.

Once the baby turned three months old, Pranati returned home, having taken a year off work to fully enjoy and settle into her role as a new mother. The house was filled with a joyful aura, with Deepa and Girish embracing their roles as doting grandparents. Friends and family often visited, drawn by the baby's infectious smile. Meanwhile, Girish had completed his work on the outhouse and was spending more and more time there, delving deeper into his spiritual studies. Shreyas had almost forgotten his trip. He was still making time for his passion, but the baby's smile would pull him back home. Pranati was planning to baby-proof the house. Though he balanced his time between his hobby and responsibilities, as Pranati started planning to baby-proof the house, it became clear that he was not entirely clued in to the needs of their growing family. He asked her to let him know if anything was needed, and he left for the office.

Deepa noticed this and began to understand what Girish had meant about Shreyas needing to be more proactive. Pranati required more than just help; Shreyas had to take initiative, foresee the needs of their household, and share the load of transforming their home to suit their baby's needs. Deepa saw the strain put on Pranati, who was frustrated with constantly giving instructions.

One afternoon, as Deepa and Pranati sat together, Deepa decided to broach the subject. "Pranati," she began gently, "our family is growing, and this house, though filled with memories, might need some changes to suit your needs. Appa and I raised our children here with elders, but times have changed. Perhaps it's time to think about modifying this house to better accommodate all of you." Pranati looked thoughtful. She hadn't considered this before, but Deepa's words made sense. The house was charming but old, and managing with a baby was becoming increasingly tedious. She remembered the trips back and forth to the bathroom, wishing there was an attached bathroom for convenience. She nodded slowly. "You're right, Amma. I hadn't thought about it, but some modifications would make things a lot easier. I'll discuss it with Shreyas and see what we can do." Shreyas was not for taking up major changes in the current home. He was thinking of an apartment. Girish was talking to a lawyer about the will. His ancestral home had to be split between his children. Laya was not in town. She told Girish and Shreyas to make the required changes for the home. Things can be settled later. Pranati loved this house. She had dreamt a thousand dreams and wanted her child to have the ancestral link. Shreyas was investing fully in the apartment. Girish and Deepa's hearts were where they were. Pranati decided to convince Shreyas to make minimal changes to the home for the present situation. That evening, Pranati brought up the topic with Shreyas. "Shreyas, I've been thinking. This house has been wonderful, but difficult to manage with the baby. Maybe we should consider some modifications, like adding an attached bathroom or making other changes to make it more baby-friendly." Shreyas looked at her, surprised. He had been very focused on the day-to-day tasks. He had not thought about the bigger picture. "You're right, Pranati. I hadn't realized how much the house needed these changes. Let's list out what we need. I'll start looking into how we can make it happen. But this is Appa's house. I need to ask him." Just then, Girish got a milk packet from the store for Pranati and came inside to put it in the fridge. He replied, "This is legally your apartment house, but my house is right now the outhouse. Don't stay under my umbrella anymore. You are now a father yourself. This is your house, and you are the head of your family. Of course, I will be there to guide you." Pranati and Shreyas were speechless at Girish's profound maturity, unconditional love, and detachment.

Over the next few weeks, Shreyas took a more active role in planning the modifications. He consulted with contractors, discussed designs with Pranati, and even took some time off work to oversee the initial stages of the renovations. Deepa and Girish provided their input, sharing their experiences and offering practical suggestions. The house slowly transformed, with new fixtures, baby-proofing measures, and additional conveniences making life easier for the growing family. Shreyas's proactive involvement brought a new dynamic to their home. He began to understand the depth of his responsibilities, not just as a father but as a supportive partner to Pranati. Their bond strengthened as they navigated this new phase together, building a safe, comfortable home filled with love for their child. The modifications made the house functional. It symbolized Shreyas's growth into a fully engaged and committed father and head of his family. Deepa and Girish decided to stay back and check on the construction activities. Pranati moved to her mother's place to avoid the dirt and disruption. Girish refrained from getting overly involved in the decisions regarding the changes, and Deepa only provided suggestions when asked. They observed with satisfaction as Pranati comfortably took over the management of the modifications. Meanwhile, Shreyas found himself grumbling about the lack of time for photography. His mind was torn between his passion, his responsibilities as a father, and his duties at the office and home. Girish noticed Shreyas struggling but chose to keep his distance, recognizing that this was a crucial part of Shreyas's learning process. Shreyas couldn't understand why his usually proactive father, always ready with suggestions, wasn't offering help. At the office, Shreyas would receive calls from the contractor and had to instruct him to call only during certain times. Choosing materials became a contentious process: what Shreyas liked, Pranati often found issues with, and vice versa. They both learned the energy that went into every decision, realizing they were no longer making choices just for themselves but had to consider each other's preferences. Compromises became the norm; Shreyas gave in on things important to Pranati, and she did the same for him. They were learning to meet halfway, understanding the essence of partnership. The home changes were completed, and they started settling in after the pooja. Pranati was surprised to see Deepa had set up a small kitchen in the outhouse. She said, "Why, Amma? What is the need?" Deepa smiled and said, "We both enjoy hot coffee. Let's have a small pantry here. Also, Pranati, Laya is recently married. She can come leisurely here, down the lane, and when she comes home to deliver another grandchild, I don't want to take up your time and space. Your hands will be full of your child and your home. It is not fair. I haven't gone out anywhere. This little physical space between us will bring us closer together. Trust me. Good fences make for good neighbors. We will take care of our grandson whenever you need us to. That is why we have planned this outhouse to be baby-friendly." Pranati was touched by Deepa's profound thoughtfulness and her foresight.

In the newly modified home, Pranati felt a newfound freedom. She felt free to change anything, invite people, and manage her home independently. Although she had this freedom before, she had always considered everyone else's opinions. Now, she realized that Deepa and Girish had moved to the outhouse to give her and Shreyas the space to build their home and raise their child according to their values. She missed having them around all the time, but her days were busier and more fulfilling as she learned new skills for managing her household. Pranati juggled bantering with maids, ensuring corners were cleaned, running the home efficiently when the baby slept or was with grandparents, doing weekly shopping, and sticking to routines with fewer eat-outs. Her mother, Sudha, once commented, "I wish I had your in-laws. My mother-in-law never understood what Deepa understood. I want to do the same when Pranav has children.". Pranati felt grateful for her in-laws, who had gracefully made room for the next generation. Shreyas's passion projects were going on. However, he observed that his irritation had decreased if he could not make time. He saw that his role had expanded forever. He was seeing his mind occupied by the office and home. He was planning for trips with the baby. There are many things to take care of to ensure a safe journey.

One day, Girish quipped, "I'm free today to pursue my passion because you are now stepping into your roles. You have a couple of decades before you can pursue only your passion. Until then, enjoy every role. Roles will expand, and responsibilities will increase.

You are capable of shouldering them. Be the leader, both at home and in the office. Learn through it all. Someday, the philosopher in you will arise. Now, let me enjoy my coffee with Dr. Prakasham. We are debating a metaphysical question." Shreyas felt a tinge of jealousy as he saw his father leave on his stroll, but quickly acknowledged that Girish deserved his quiet time. He had left large shoes for Shreyas to fill. Smiling, Shreyas thought, "Why not enjoy my new role?" As his father said, there was a lot to learn before the philosopher in him could arise. Embracing this journey, Shreyas felt more settled and ready to face the challenges and joys ahead.

Your Soul has Chosen its Way

Your soul has chosen its way,
You can't complain, come what may.
Friends, spouse, and kin all play their part,
To mold your soul, to shape your heart.

If faults in others you always find,
And agitation fills your mind,
It's not the world that needs a fix,
But you, dear soul, in this mix.
The world's a mirror, reflecting true,
What lies within, comes back to you.
Thank them as Gurus, learn and grow,
Release the karma, let it go.

The mind will see what it desires,
Detach from judgments, quench the fires.
Let flaws in others simply be,
Their burdens, are not for you to see.
Life is short, spread love, be kind,
Leave all bitterness behind.

When you stand at heaven's gate,
Let your deeds be proud and great.
You're just a channel, never the doer,
He moves through you; His love is pure.
Surrender to His grand design,
In every life, His light will shine.